KU-787-720

THE RESCUE OF RAVENWOOD

NATASHA FARRANT

faber

For my parents, who taught me to love books
and the natural world.

First published in 2023
by Faber & Faber Limited
Bloomsbury House,
74–77 Great Russell Street,
London WC1B 3DA
faber.co.uk

Typeset in Garamond by MRules
Printed by CPI Group (UK) Ltd, Croydon CR0 4YY

All rights reserved
Text © Natasha Farrant, 2023

The right of Natasha Farrant to be identified as author
of this work has been asserted in accordance with Section 77
of the Copyright, Designs and Patents Act 1988

*This book is sold subject to the condition that it shall not, by way of trade or
otherwise, be lent, resold, hired out or otherwise circulated without the publisher's
prior consent in any form of binding or cover other than that in which it is
published and without a similar condition including this condition
being imposed on the subsequent purchaser*

A CIP record for this book is available from the British Library

ISBN 978–0–571–34878–7

MIX
Paper | Supporting
responsible forestry
FSC® C171272

Printed and bound in the UK on FSC paper in line with our continuing
commitment to ethical business practices, sustainability and the environment.
For further information see faber.co.uk/environmental-policy

2 4 6 8 10 9 7 5 3 1

'*Sometimes the beauty of the world can take your breath away.*'

from *The Children of Castle Rock*

PROLOGUE

B ea and Raffy came to Ravenwood when they were babies, and they loved it straight away.

Surrounded by ancient woods in the north of England, perched between the Ashby valley and the sea, the house and its surrounding outhouses sit on the highest point for miles around. Ever since the Iron Age, people have lived here – early farmers, Roman soldiers. Viking settlers. Four hundred years ago, give or take, a rich merchant built his manor here, and named it after the great birds which circled its cliffs and woodlands. The manor was burned down in one war, rebuilt, bombed in another war, rebuilt again. The new house is square, white and a lot scruffier than it was, but that's not the point.

I

The point is, it's a place people come back to.

A place people fight for.

Bea came first, Ravenwood being her family home. On the day our story begins, it was owned by her father and her two uncles, who inherited it from their parents. Alex Pembury – Bea's father, the eldest of the three brothers – lived in London with Bea's mother Ingrid, and worked in finance. Jack Pembury, the middle brother, lived in Central America, doing nobody knew quite what. Leo Pembury, the youngest, lived at Ravenwood and was an artist. He made giant installations from wood and old junk in one of Ravenwood's three barns, which he had turned into a studio. To his brothers' astonishment, people sometimes actually paid for his work, though never very much.

The last few decades had been peaceful up on the hill, but today the house was once again under attack, not from planes or armies but from the weather. Last night, a late summer storm smashed an oak tree through the kitchen roof. On the morning we join them, Leo – like so many before him – is clearing up. Alex is driving from London to inspect the damage. Bea is in her baby seat in the back.

Alex had loved going home when he first moved to London, but since his parents died Ravenwood mainly exhausted him. With its big, draughty rooms, its weather and its problematic trees, the old place was a drain – on his money, his time, his energy. He never came any more unless he had to. But now here he was, off to sort out the latest problem when he should have been at work, taking his small baby with him because the childminder was sick and Ingrid was having one of her bad days. He was tired – so tired. Worried, too, and prickly with resentment at having to make this journey.

And yet . . .

Shortly before lunch, he drove through the village of Ashby-under-Raven and turned on to the unpaved track which led up to Ravenwood. At the top of the hill, just where the track flattened, there was a gap in the trees. Out of habit, Alex stopped and opened the window, the way he used to when he still loved the place, to catch that first lungful of sea air.

The wind rushed into the car.

Bea, who had slept all the way from London, woke up.

Alex drove through the old iron gate (rusted, in need of repair, guarded on either side by a moss-covered stone raven on a crumbling pillar), parked beneath the old ash tree and looked up.

'Hello, Ygg,' he said.

Even now and even for Alex, it was a magical tree. Four hundred years old, thirty metres tall and almost as wide across, it stood by the entrance of Ravenwood like a guardian spirit. As a boy, Leo had named it Yggdrasil, like the tree of life in Viking myths. 'Because Vikings used to live here,' Leo had said. 'And it *is* full of life.' As if to prove a point, a raven had taken off from one of the top branches in a great beating of wings, and from then on it had become Yggdrasil for everybody. Peering up, Alex saw that the platform their father had built for his brothers and him to play on when they were boys was still there, defying all safety regulations, about five metres up. A frayed rope ladder hung along the trunk. Just for a moment, Alex considered climbing it . . .

He shook his head. He had long given up climbing trees. Instead, he got out of the car, opened the back door, took Bea out of her seat and went in search of his brother.

Years later, Leo would enjoy describing the first time he saw Bea at Ravenwood.

'The mess!' he would say. 'The roof smashed, tiles everywhere, shattered glass, broken branches and in the middle of it all, like a miniature queen, Bea gobbling it all up with her eyes on stalks.'

'I was *not* like a queen and I do *not* gobble,' Bea would say, tossing her long red hair.

'I picked her up,' Leo would say, 'and I carried her across the garden to look at the sea. It was one of those grey days, you know, when there seems to be no light, but then the sun came out and the sea was turned to gold. And little miss madam here, hardly bigger than a kitten . . .'

'A kitten!'

'. . . stretched out her arms like she was saying *all*

of this is mine! Even then, she knew exactly what she wanted.'

Back then, the brothers argued. Tedious, grown-up arguments about insurance papers and new kitchens. Alex said, if only you'd cut down that tree. Leo said, how was I to know it would fall. And so on and so forth. It isn't really interesting.

What *is* interesting is that while Leo and Alex argued, out on the tree-smashed terrace, Bea gazed at the clouds scooting across the washed-out sky and tilted her head to the song of a blackbird.

That when they moved indoors and Leo laid her on the living-room rug, she watched entranced as a spider spun its web between two ceiling beams.

And that when at last the arguing was done and Alex tried to put her back in the car, she refused to be put in her seat, arching her back and screaming until her face went purple.

'What am I supposed to do?' asked Alex, close to tears himself.

'Here, give her to me,' said Leo.

Bea stopped crying as soon as she was in Leo's arms.

Leo laughed and said, 'I think she wants to stay.'

It was the perfect solution, Leo liked to say. Alex so tired, Ingrid not well, the childminder also sick. Him all alone in the big house.

'Just for a few days,' Alex said to Ingrid on the phone. 'Until everything is better.'

'But what does Leo know about babies?' Ingrid worried.

'About as much as I do,' said Alex, which was almost true.

'And you're sure she really likes it there?'

'I think she really does.'

'Just until everything is better, then,' said Ingrid after a pause.

And Bea stayed.

Bea cooed as Alex took the bag of baby things out of the car. She gurgled as he drove away. Leo laid her on a blanket on the terrace near where the tree had fallen and she pumped her arms and legs like a miniature gymnast. He walked away to continue his clearing.

She began to cry again.

Leo tried to prepare a bottle of milk in the microwave, but the bottle exploded. He tried to feed

Bea apple sauce, but she spat it out. He gave her a rusk, but she hurled it away.

Clearly, babies were more complicated than he had thought.

In the end, he drove to the village for help, with Bea wedged between his legs because he couldn't work out how to fit the car seat.

And this was the best bit.

The elderly volunteers who worked in the shop were fond of Leo, whom they had known all his life. They did their best for him. 'Have you tried changing her nappy?' one asked, and 'maybe she's hungry' said another, and 'why don't we all try singing to her?' suggested a third.

And then (Leo would say), an angel appeared.

'Try this.'

A new voice, quiet but assured. A young woman nobody knew stood by the noticeboard at the shop's entrance – about his age, dark-skinned, with a halo of soft curls, dressed in a city raincoat, with a rucksack on her back and a sleeping baby in a pushchair.

She held out what looked like a tube of toothpaste.

'It's teething gel,' she said. 'Put a bit on your finger and rub it on her gums.'

Leo did as he was told. Bea instantly stopped crying.

Resisting the urge to kiss the miraculous stranger's feet, Leo said, 'How can I ever thank you?'

The stranger nodded towards the noticeboard. 'I don't suppose you have a room?'

Leo didn't think twice.

'I do have a room!' he cried. 'I have many, many rooms!'

'It's true,' said one of the volunteers. 'He does.'

'Please stay!' said Leo, wildly. 'I so badly need help.'

'That's also true,' said another volunteer.

The stranger didn't answer at once but gazed at him with her head on one side, calm dark eyes appraising him like they were looking right into his soul.

Leo prayed his soul was good enough.

At last, the stranger smiled. 'Thank you,' she said. 'We would like that very much. Just for a few days.'

That was how it started.

Her name was Martha and her baby was Raffy and none of them could know then that a few days would turn into a week then a month until, eleven years later, they were all still living at Ravenwood. That Martha would become a teacher at the Ashby primary school, that she and Leo would fall in love, that together they would turn Ravenwood into a place where everyone was welcome, that over time they would let nature take over the garden until it became a wilderness where birds and animals also came in droves. That out of the fallen oak which had smashed the kitchen, Leo would build a life-size model of a Viking longboat complete with mast and oars, to commemorate this day.

Over the years, Leo would tell how, as he drove his van back up the hill with Martha beside him holding the babies, Raffy woke and took Bea's hand.

Martha would smile when Leo got to that bit and say they have never really let go.

PART ONE

ELEVEN YEARS LATER

CHAPTER ONE

For whole days leading up to the summer holidays, all Raffy could talk about was the great crested newt.

It was discovered by accident on the last Saturday before the end of term, when a boy called Ernie Smith kicked his football into the village pond, rushed in after it, stumbled on his way out and – bam! There was the newt like a miniature dragon, with a fiery underbelly and spikes on its dark green back, hiding behind a stone.

On the whole, the people of Ashby-under-Raven rejoiced. The Nature Society celebrated with tea and extra biscuits. The science lead in the primary school made worksheets. The librarian wrote a blog piece.

Only two people were cross.

The first was the pub landlord, who had been planning to build a car park on the meadow next to the pond. Now that there was a great crested newt, he was not allowed to do it, because the great crested newt, said the man from the council who came to inspect it, was Rare and thus Protected. Which meant, he explained, No Building Anywhere Near It.

'Building near the Newt,' he said, 'would Destroy its Habitat.'

The second cross person was Raffy.

To be clear: Raffy wasn't cross with the newt itself. Raffy loved the newt, as he loved all living creatures. He not only loved it, he admired it – this tiny amphibian which could single-handedly stop a whole car park being built. Raffy, who was small himself, thought this was marvellous. He just wished the newt hadn't let itself be discovered by Ernie Smith.

Unlike Raffy, Ernie Smith cared nothing about nature. All Ernie Smith cared about was football. Ernie Smith, until Raffy had corrected him, had *actually thought the newt was a frog.* Basically, Raffy was jealous.

All through that final week ever at Ashby Primary, when all their classmates talked about were parties and Meadowbanks, the new school twenty miles away in town that most of them would be going to in the autumn, Raffy grumbled.

During the holidays, he muttered, he was going to find an even rarer newt, in their very own pond up at Ravenwood. Possibly even a species no one had ever heard of before.

No other conversation was possible. One way or another, the subject would always come back to the newt, until late on a Wednesday evening something happened which was even more momentous: Jack Pembury called from Costa Rica to say that for the first time in ten years he was returning to England. He would be at Ravenwood at the weekend. Bea's parents were coming too, before setting off to Venice for a sailing holiday.

Everything was turned upside down. Suddenly, there were sheets to wash, beds to make, flowers to cut and put into vases, food to be bought and meals prepared. Despite Martha's best efforts to keep things tidy, Ravenwood usually existed in a state of gentle chaos, but Alex and Ingrid liked *order*. And there had been an awkwardness last year with Jack when he asked Leo for money. He and Leo had barely spoken since. Now was a chance to make things right between them, starting with Jack's old room, which despite the faded curtains and the hole in the ceiling must be made as welcoming as possible.

Most of all, though, there was Bea to look after.

Over the years, visits from Bea's parents had developed a pattern. They came for her birthday, for Christmas and sometimes for the weekend. Every time, though they never said as much out loud, the residents of Ravenwood felt the pressure to be on their best behaviour. It wasn't just about tidying the house. It was more that Ingrid was so easily upset. No one had forgotten Bea's ninth birthday lunch, when Ingrid had run from the table in tears because she thought Bea didn't like her present, or the Christmas when she hadn't left her room because the tree was already decorated when she arrived. On each occasion, she and Alex had cut their visit short and driven back to London, with no explanation except a terse *I think we'd better go* from Alex. And while these visits were extremes, and some went by without incident, this one threatened to be complicated.

Until recently, Bea had been fairly robust about her parents. Yes, her family situation was unusual, but Leo and Martha and Raffy and Ravenwood more than made up for her parents' absence, and Bea usually shrugged off the discomfort of their stay within a few days. But in the spring, something had changed. Alex had called out of the blue to say that he and Ingrid were going to France for Easter, and that they wanted Bea to go with them.

Leo and Martha had been worried about letting her go, Bea had been confused and Raffy, who had never been separated from her before, had cried. But, 'They *are* her parents,' Martha had said to Leo, curled up together on the living-room sofa when they thought the children had gone to bed. 'We can't very well refuse.'

And so Bea had gone.

She had never been anywhere with her parents and

it was her first trip abroad. At the beginning it was wonderful. They had driven the car on to the ferry and spent the crossing on deck wrapped in shawls, eating cake as sunlight glinted off the waves. On their first night, they had stayed in a castle and she and Ingrid had read together, snuggled in her bed. The next morning for breakfast there had been hot chocolate and homemade jam in a room with tall windows overlooking a garden.

'Isn't this heaven? Just like a fairy tale!' Ingrid had said, and Bea had agreed because eating breakfast in a pretty room with her smiling parents had felt like a strange and wonderful thing, the strangest, most wonderful thing of all being how happy they seemed to be with her.

She had not realised, until it happened, how much she had always wanted this.

The fairy tale ended abruptly, with a pair of kittens tumbling into the room. Bea laughed and said she wished she could take them home with her, Ingrid began to cry, and she didn't stop until the holiday, like the birthday and Christmas visits, was cut short.

This time, Bea was not robust. This time, something precious was lost. There had been a sea crossing and cake, stories and cuddles. Hot chocolate and jam and fairy tales. This time, when her parents left her, Bea had wept buckets in Martha's arms.

'It's not your fault,' Martha had said when at last Bea stopped. 'You've not done anything wrong.'

'I must have,' whispered Bea. 'Or why didn't they keep me?'

And to this, Martha had no answer.

Leo arrived then with tea, and gingerbread baked specially for Bea by her friend Maisie's mum, and later they had gone to the cove. Life at Ravenwood had resumed its course, but Bea never was convinced she hadn't done something wrong.

Being Bea, she pretended she was fine and because they loved her, the others pretended to believe her. But they weren't fooled. There was a new intensity now to Martha's hugs. Leo, who was so often distracted, grew more attentive. And Raffy, who had always worshipped Bea as a sort of superhero and missed her so much while she was away he struggled to get out of bed, discovered in himself a new protectiveness. A boy who built shelters for hedgehogs and would go out of his way not to tread on an ant, he found himself often daydreaming of just what he would do to Bea's parents if they ever hurt her again ...

Now, as this first visit since the terrible French trip loomed, Bea felt sick with apprehension. What should she do? Should she apologise for whatever it was she had done wrong? Would Ingrid cry, or would she be as she was on that first happy day of their trip? Bea, who was normally so noisy, forever stomping up and down stairs shouting for things she had lost, thumping on the piano, singing in the shower – went very quiet.

Leo, Martha and Raffy did what they could to help her. Despite the soaring temperatures – they were into the second week of a blazing heatwave – Leo built a fire in the cove to cook sausages and marshmallows. Martha kept her busy with chores to stop her from thinking about her parents. And Raffy almost completely stopped complaining about the newt, instead keeping up a steady stream of chatter about anything but her parents, as he helped Bea with the chores.

The first day of the holidays dawned, bright and sunny. A morning for a celebratory swim, perhaps, or exploring the woods to decide where to build a den, or stealing strawberries from the kitchen garden.

Bea spent it indoors, now attempting to tidy her formidably messy bedroom, now trying to read on the sofa, now taking over the bathroom floor to make a mess of painting her toenails. Just after lunch, Leo set off to the station in the van to fetch the visitors. Bea, having decided to wait for her parents at home, threw herself into the old armchair in the kitchen and wondered aloud if she should have gone with him.

Martha, putting away the last of the lunch things, said, 'Let's go for a swim.'

Swimming at Ravenwood was considered a cure for everything, but Bea just looked at Martha as if she were mad.

'I can't *swim*!' she said. 'I feel so sick I might actually drown.'

Raffy, with a longing glance towards the woods, said, 'We could ...'

'I'm not looking for a newt,' snapped Bea.

'Ygg, then,' said Raffy.

Bea sighed. 'Ygg.'

Out they went through the flower meadow to the old ash tree, where they climbed a new rope ladder to the platform Leo had rebuilt a few years ago to replace the one he and his brothers had played on as boys. Beneath them the garden, the valley and even the sea shimmered in the heat, but up here the air was cool. Bea and Raffy lay on their backs and looked up through still, heavy branches at the sky.

'I've been wondering something,' said Bea. 'If things hadn't gone so wrong in France, do you think my parents would have asked me to go to Italy with them?'

Raffy stared at her, astounded.

'Do you *want* to go to Italy with them?' he asked.

'Of course not,' she said scornfully, and Raffy felt weak with relief, because the idea of Bea going away again was unthinkable.

'It will be nice to meet your uncle,' he said, steering the subject to safer waters. 'We can ask him about Costa Rica. Did you know it has more biodiversity than any other country on Earth? I read about it. They have nearly two hundred different sorts of amphibians, including newts...'

'Raffy, could we not talk about newts?'

'Sorry,' he said. 'I forgot.'

'Tell me about the tree house instead.'

Raffy beamed, instantly cheered. Before the newt, the tree house had been his top summer project. He had been planning it for months with Nick, a retired carpenter from the village Leo had befriended after Nick's wife died, and who often came to Ravenwood. Nick had already sawn planks from a fallen beech tree. Over the past weeks, Raffy had helped to plane them till they were smooth, and oil them so they were weatherproof. Now it was ready to assemble in Yggdrasil.

'We're going to build it right here, but we won't cover the platform completely. We'll keep a bit open so we can still sit out. The cabin will have a pitched roof, and inside we're going to make bunks so we can sleep up here – four bunks, so friends can stay over too – and there'll be a big window over the valley, and we might see the barn owl...'

Bea grunted. The barn owl which had recently arrived at Ravenwood was already the stuff of legend, having been heard often but never actually seen.

'What if we need a wee?' she asked.

'There'll be a bucket.'

'A bucket!'

Raffy grinned at Bea's shout of laughter.

'Nick says, we could have a pulley system, to hoist things up and down. For the wee bucket, but also for provisions. There'll be storage under the bunks and we're going to make shelves too. Nick says...'

On he talked, and Bea grew peaceful.

Two days, she thought, then her parents would leave. They would fly off to Italy for their sailing holiday, and *she* could throw herself into a glorious Ravenwood summer without worrying about them. She would swim every day in the cove and when it was built she would sleep in the tree house. Maisie and other friends would come for swims and picnics. In a few weeks, when the plums ripened, they would all climb into the trees to shake them out on to sheets held out by the pensioners from the retirement home who helped in the garden.

This was all Bea wanted, before starting at Meadowbanks. All she *needed*. Calm. Reassurance. Everything just as it always had been, as soon as her parents were gone.

Oh dear.

Well, read on.

Raffy talked and Bea was peaceful. But then at last, in the distance, beyond birdsong and Raffy's voice and the murmuring breeze, came the unmistakable rattle of Leo's van. Bea and Raffy crawled to the edge of the platform and lay on their fronts to watch as it bounced along the track up from the valley.

'Should we go down?' asked Raffy.

But Bea felt sick again. 'Let's wait.'

The van was through the gate now, parking directly beneath them. Bea's throat tightened. The driver's door opened. Leo climbed out and looked up.

They waited, but no one else appeared.

Slowly, Bea sat up. Her head was reeling. She sat on her hands, pressing them into the wood of the platform to steady herself.

Beside her, Raffy clenched his fists in sympathy.

'I'm so sorry, Bea.' Leo ran his hands through his hair, the way he always did when he was troubled. 'They didn't come. Did Martha not tell you? I sent her a message.'

Bea tried to speak, but no sound came out. Raffy looked at her, feeling helpless.

'Mum went for a swim,' he told Leo. 'What happened? Why aren't they here?'

Something was pressing into Bea's chest. She wriggled, but it still hurt. Inside her, she registered dully. The pain was inside her.

What had she done that was so awful her parents hadn't even come?

Dimly, she heard Leo reply to Raffy's question. He hadn't received Alex's message until he got to the station, something had come up at the last minute, they all had to stay in London. Jack was coming later but there was no time now for her parents to visit before they left.

'But –' here, ever so slightly, Leo faltered – 'I have a surprise!'

He went back to the van and opened the passenger door. Bea and Raffy both blinked.

A girl had climbed out of the van and was looking up at them, her expression at once hopeful and nervous – about their age and Bea's height, neat, dainty, with light brown skin and dark hair arranged in two shoulder-length braids, smartly dressed in a flared blue skirt and a red vest, a canvas satchel slung across her body and silver sandals on her feet. Bea, already feeling bad, suddenly felt worse, very aware of her own scruffy denim cut-offs, her grubby trainers and not very clean T-shirt.

Raffy was just baffled.

'Come and say hello!' called Leo, waving them down. 'This is Noa! She's coming to stay for the holidays!'

And the summer took another turn.

CHAPTER TWO

Noa's mother Agnes went to the evening sculpture classes Leo ran in town, he explained once Bea and Raffy had climbed down from Ygg. She was also a doctor. There had been an earthquake in a faraway country, followed by a flood, and now there were outbreaks of a disease in the camps where people were living who had lost their homes, and Noa's mother had been asked to help.

'The earthquake was in the news,' Leo said, as if this somehow explained everything. 'Agnes was supposed to fly out tonight, but when I bumped into her and Noa in town, Agnes said she couldn't go, because there was nobody to look after Noa. So I said she could stay with us!'

He paused, expectantly, and tried not to wince under Bea's hard stare.

'Cool!' said Raffy, just a bit too late.

'Excellent!' said Leo, just a bit too heartily.

Bea continued to stare. Raffy shuffled his feet. Noa, looking mortified, began to scratch her wrist. Leo ran his hands through his hair again, overcome as was so often the case by the feeling that he hadn't properly thought through his spontaneous gesture, and looked around for the only person who could help.

'Let's go and see if Martha's back,' he said.

They found her in the kitchen, making tea. Fresh from the shower after her swim, she had not yet read Leo's message but when he explained – his hair really a wild mess now – that his brothers and sister-in-law had failed to arrive, that Jack was coming this evening and that meanwhile Noa was here instead, she responded to the situation with all of her usual warm practicality. First with a quick hug to comfort Bea, who still had not uttered a word since Leo's return. Then with another hug for Noa, the offer of cake, tea, a drink of squash. When Noa – also apparently incapable of speech – shook her head, she took her upstairs to the sunny little box room squeezed in between Bea and Raffy's rooms at the end of the landing, showed her the closet and chest of drawers where she could put away her things, fetched her a beach towel from the airing cupboard and then, with the kindly briskness which her family knew brooked no disobedience, ordered Bea and Raffy to take Noa for a swim.

'I could murder my brothers,' said Leo, when the children were out of earshot.

Even though she whole-heartedly agreed, Martha said that wouldn't help.

Bea did not behave well.

She didn't wait for the others on the way to the cove. Instead, despite the heat, she ran as fast as she could through the meadow towards the cliff where the path down to the water began. Behind her, she could hear Raffy and Noa struggling to keep up, Raffy trying to make up for Bea's rudeness by pointing out the names of flowers, the goldfinches feeding on teasel heads, the butterflies which had finally returned to Ravenwood this summer after twenty years' absence.

Bea bared her teeth in a silent scream. How could Leo do this? She knew how much he enjoyed sharing Ravenwood – with Nick from the village, the old people who came to garden, Bea and Raffy's friends. He was always organising events, like carols at Christmas, the big bonfire for Guy Fawkes, apple pressing in the autumn. But to bring a stranger for the whole summer? On the day her parents . . .

The pain in Bea's chest grew sharper and she ran faster. She didn't want to think about her parents.

At the fork in the path – left for the woods, right towards the cliff – Bea slowed and glanced over her shoulder. The others were walking now, side by side, Raffy still pointing things out.

She sped up again. She didn't stop until she came to the place which, more than any other, she considered her own: Leo's Viking longboat, built from the storm-felled oak which had brought her to Ravenwood as a baby, poised like a bird on the edge of the cliff in an oval of sand, its hull shaped like folded wings, its prow a graceful dragon head. Skidbládnir, Leo had called it, the name of the greatest of Viking ships, which could fly in the air or sail on the sea, with planks so thin it could be folded into a pocket. Bea had loved it since she was a baby. She slid her hands now on to the dragon's neck and leaned her forehead against the hull.

Usually Skidbládnir calmed her. Why wasn't it now?

She heard the others arrive behind her but did not turn, bristling as Raffy began to tell the story of the longboat and their arrival at Ravenwood. When he got to the part where she refused to be strapped into her car seat, she could take no more and finally whipped round.

'Let's go!' she said.

Raffy's eyes widened in shock at her rudeness and Noa's in what looked like anger, but they still followed her. Bea felt a spiteful surge of triumph.

She stopped at the edge of the cliff path, letting Noa take in the perfect horseshoe shape of the cove beneath them, its water bright blue in the clear still day, its fringe of flat grey rocks gleaming in the sun.

There was a choice to make now.

She could be kind.

Or she could not.

'There's a proper beach at low tide to swim from, but when it's high like now . . .' Bea pointed to the far end of the cove, where dark cliffs fell dramatically to the water. 'When it's high tide, we jump from there.'

Almost imperceptibly, Noa gulped.

'Or we can swim from the rocks,' Raffy offered, with a little frown at Bea. 'We don't *have* to jump if you don't want to. It *is* quite high.'

Bea glared at him. 'Your choice,' she said to Noa.

It wasn't a choice though; it was a challenge. Just for a second, Bea saw the other girl's eyes blaze. She was almost glad, because she knew she was being unfair. But then Noa looked away.

'You go,' she said. 'I don't really feel like swimming.'

It would be nice to write that Bea backed down then, and suggested doing something different with Noa – show her round the woods, maybe, or take her up into Yggdrasil. But she didn't. She ran straight off again, down the steep path, then across the cove to the cliffs. Raffy hesitated, torn between loyalty to Bea and politeness to their guest. When he made up his mind and followed Bea, she gave a grunt of satisfaction but did not look back.

At the foot of the cliffs she stripped down to her swimsuit and, leaving her clothes on the rocks, began to climb. Raffy cast a worried look to where Noa still stood where they had left her then pulled himself up after Bea.

'You know, Noa's actually quite nice,' he said, when they stopped at the ledge from which they usually jumped.

'Go back and look after her, then,' said Bea. 'If you like her so much.'

'I'm just saying we shouldn't have left …'

But Bea was climbing again.

'Where are you going?' squeaked Raffy.

'Higher!'

The next ledge was only about a metre above their usual spot, but when Bea turned to look down it seemed much more. She had never dared jump from so high before. Could she do it now? She pressed her back into the cliff, palms flat against the solid rock, feeling as though invisible hands were wringing out her insides.

How very dark the water was …

For about half a second, she thought of backing

down. But Raffy was watching from the ledge below and above them on the edge of the cliff was Noa, her stupid skirt fluttering in the breeze, the strap of her stupid satchel a dark line across her red top, and somewhere in London were Bea's parents who couldn't be bothered to see her before going on their stupid holiday, and most of all in her chest there was this pain she didn't know what to do with.

She knew this cove, though, this sea. Where to jump, and how, and when. She stepped to the front of the ledge. Waited, as Leo had taught her, for the calm between two gentle swells then

screamed

and

jumped.

She hit the water like an arrow, straight and true. The world exploded into a cloud of bubbles. For a few seconds she hung suspended beneath the surface. Then, with a rapid beating of legs, she propelled herself upwards and burst back out into the open air.

'I did it!' she yelled. 'Did you see, Raffy? I did it!'

Sometimes, all you can do is jump.

*

Noa turned away after watching Bea's leap and walked back towards the longboat, frowning as she tried to piece the day back together.

How had she agreed to this?

There had been the earthquake, like Leo said, then the flood and the disease. The call from Mum's old boss asking would she help, and Mum being Mum saying yes, 'because it was important'. Noa didn't actually mind that bit. Secretly, she was proud of her mother. What she *did* mind was being asked to stay with Dad, in the house where he now lived with his new girlfriend Tamsin and her horrible toddler twin girls.

It would be much better, Noa had said, if Dad would move in with her, in the flat where she now lived with Mum.

'On his own,' Noa had specified.

To which Tamsin, in a long conversation with Mum, had said no.

'I suppose they're a family now,' Mum had said, too nobly in Noa's opinion. 'They don't split up.'

Which was rubbish, because families did split up. That was precisely the point.

Until now, since her parents' separation, Noa had always been *nice*. Seeing how stressed her mother was and knowing that money was short, she had not complained about moving to a different part of town when they sold the old house, or about how lonely she was at the new school they sent her to. Every other Saturday, she went out for the day with Dad. He had shown her photographs of the bedroom he and Tamsin had prepared for her in their home, and though the sight of it made her want to smash the screen, she had said how nice it looked.

'I don't want to leave Mum on her own, though,' she had added to get out of actually staying with him, and until the earthquake-flood-plague thing, everyone had respected that.

Now though, things were different.

'There is nowhere else for you to stay,' Mum had said, and Noa had finally put her foot down.

'If you make me stay with them,' she told Mum, 'I will run away.'

She had then asked to stay with her older sister Elva, who was an art student in Bristol and Noa's favourite person in the world, but neither of her parents would hear of that. Firstly, because Elva did things like get arrested for spraying paintings of polar bears on to buildings during climate marches and was 'not sufficiently responsible to look after a child'. Secondly, because Elva was actually in Paris on an art scholarship for the summer.

That was where they had got to when they had run into Leo near the station, and he quite extraordinarily invited Noa to stay at Ravenwood. Mum had laughed at first, but then Leo had said no really, he meant it, and Mum had looked sort of hopeful but worried at once, and even though Noa couldn't actually believe Mum would leave her with virtual strangers for *the whole summer*, she had found herself agreeing too, *because she was so nice*.

After that, everything had gone very fast and now here she was, miles from any person or any place she knew.

For weeks.

For a moment, glimpsing them on that amazing platform in the tree, she had hoped Bea and Raffy might be different from the children at school, but clearly she had been wrong. She ran her hand along the curve of the longboat's hull until she came to the prow.

'Who needs friends anyway,' she said to the scaly dragon head.

Before everything fell apart, Noa had been popular. Then she had tried to make friends at her new school, but Year Six was a stupid time to move. Maybe she should have taken up Bea's challenge, impressed her and gone to the cliff to jump. But Bea was so angry, and the cliffs looked so high ... Raffy seemed sweet, but he clearly took his lead from Bea. Noa could have done it. She could have gritted her teeth and forced herself to jump, and she could have done it with a smile on her face too, pretending she didn't mind or hadn't noticed Bea's hostility. But it would have been hard, and Noa was so very tired of trying.

Still, she told herself bracingly, as she had tried to do all year, there was no point moping. She was just going to have to put on a brave face as usual and make the most of it. Right now, that meant exploring this strange boat. She stood on tiptoe to look over the side, glanced over her shoulder to check nobody was watching, then climbed in.

She sat down on one of the benches, but the wood under her bare thighs was too hot, and she slipped quickly into the shade at the bottom of the boat. At the base of the mast, there was a locker, which she opened after a brief struggle with a stiff bolt. Inside was a lantern made of multicoloured glass, a candle, a box of matches, a deck of cards, cushions, a set of metal tumblers. Skidbládnir wasn't just a display piece, then. People actually used it, came here to play games and eat and drink. She closed her eyes to imagine what that must be like.

Wonderful, she thought. Really wonderful.

A loud caw above her made her jump. Looking up, she saw a raven watching from the top of the mast. Noa caught her breath. She had read a lot of books over the past year, including myths and fairy tales. Weren't ravens supposed to be messengers from other worlds? The great Norse god Odin had two, who flew around the world for him, gathering information. Witches also used them as spies. What was this one trying to tell her?

'Don't move,' she whispered.

Slowly, so as not to alarm the great bird, she pulled

the strap of her satchel over her head, then slid out her sketchbook and box of pencils. For a few seconds, she sat still, her hands on the open page, feeling the smoothness of the paper. Books and drawing had got her through the past year. Books and drawing would help her now.

Another caw and the raven flew off, its silhouette growing smaller against the sun. Noa watched it leave with regret, then turned back to the page, tapping her pencil against her teeth.

How would she draw this place? Skidbládnir, the raven? Raffy, Bea?

A smile hovered on her lips as an idea began to take shape. With quick, clever strokes, before it disappeared, she began.

Far away in London, Jack Pembury said goodbye to his brother and sister-in-law and set off for Ravenwood alone in a hire car. He had some regrets about what he had just done, but not enough to stop him. He had come back for a reason, and he had a plan.

A plan he had just set in motion.

CHAPTER THREE

Bea and Raffy stayed at the cove all afternoon, jumping and swimming then jumping some more (though not from the higher ledge – that, Bea said, was a *once only* sort of jump). When the tide began to go out and a crescent of damp sand appeared on the shore, they lay in the shallows, rolled by the lapping ebb and flow of the water. They spoke little, but when they did it was about gentle things, like what books they would take up to the tree house when it was built, and the white doe Raffy had seen recently in the woods, drinking at the pond with her fawn. They did not talk about Bea's parents, and if Raffy still felt bad about abandoning Noa, he kept the feeling to himself. By the time they walked back across the meadow in the long shadows of the early evening, Bea still felt sore, but she was calm again. At the fork in the path, they looked along the edge of the woods towards Yggdrasil and saw a new car parked by the raven gate.

Jack Pembury had arrived.

'Ready?' asked Raffy.

Bea took a deep breath. 'Ready.'

'There she is!'

Jack had been sitting on the terrace with Leo on the broken chairs which passed for garden furniture, but he got up when Bea and Raffy joined them.

'Let me look at you!' He held Bea at arms' length, his hands digging into her shoulders, clearly unsure how to deal with a child, playing the part of approachable uncle. Bea resisted the temptation to squirm away from him. As she tried to meet his gaze full on, she had the strangest feeling that she was looking at Leo and her father as well, a sunkissed, muscular version with the faintest hint of a mid-Atlantic accent – smarter than Leo (which was not difficult) but more relaxed than Alex (also not difficult).

'My, you've grown! I suppose you *were* only a baby when I left! And this is Raffy, am I right? Martha's boy? Good to make your acquaintance, young man! I have just met your mother and believe me, she has prepared us a feast!'

Raffy, unsure how to respond to such an onslaught of heartiness, stared at Jack's feet (tanned, strong, clad in sturdy hiking sandals) and muttered a shy 'hello'.

Leo, looking rather tired, said, 'You'd better go and have a shower. Make it quick though, we're eating soon.'

It was, for the most part, a lovely evening. There was an awkward moment when Bea and Raffy came back downstairs and found Noa laying the table, neat as a pin and her expression inscrutable. Raffy wanted to apologise but didn't know how or exactly what for. Bea, a little ashamed of her earlier behaviour, wanted to be friendly but couldn't think what to say. But then Martha ordered Bea to fill a jug of water and Raffy to fetch the salad from the fridge, and the awkwardness passed. Leo came in with Jack and poured drinks. Martha brought food to the table and she had indeed prepared a feast – her signature lasagne was rich, the freshly pulled lettuce crisp, the home-grown strawberries sweet, the chocolate cake light and melting. As they ate, they began to relax. Leo set aside his irritation with his brothers, and he and Jack began to swap stories of growing up at Ravenwood. Despite a hint of tension in the air, it was almost possible to forget that two other people should have been with them at the table.

Almost.

After dinner, in the deepening twilight, as birdsong gave way to the call of the invisible barn owl, Leo prepared a tea tray and they all went out to the terrace.

'What is your house like, Jack, in Costa Rica?' Martha asked, when Leo had poured everyone a cup.

Jack didn't answer straight away but took a cigarillo from his shirt pocket, then pulled a heavy, rectangular brass lighter from his jeans.

Leo smiled. 'Dad's lighter!'

'Always,' Jack said, smiling back.

Oh yes, it was all very lovely . . .

Jack was still smiling as he struck the lighter, the light cast from the flame throwing shadows around him. He lit the cigarillo then, blowing out a plume of smoke, sat back and began to talk. He was a good storyteller.

'The house where I live,' he said, 'is paradise. It's always cool, even on the hottest days, and there is a swimming pool fed by a natural waterfall. Monkeys come into the garden from the forest . . .'

Raffy forced himself to overcome his shyness. 'What sort of monkeys?' he asked.

'Capuchin and howler, mainly. Squirrel monkeys if you're lucky.'

Raffy gave a groan of envy. One day, he promised himself, he would see monkeys in the wild. 'What other animals are there?'

'Oh, so many! Tree frogs and parakeets, and so many hummingbirds. We put out sugar water for them, and once I counted almost a hundred, all different colours and sizes, like flying jewels.'

'What colours?' Raffy was completely captivated now.

'Every colour.'

'And what sizes?'

'From as small as my thumb to as big as your hand,' laughed Jack.

Raffy looked at his hands, imagining them as birds.

On Jack talked. About the tiny frogs which slept clinging to the underside of leaves, and the family of capybaras which came to the garden at dusk to drink from the pool, and iridescent butterflies the size of saucers, and the sloth who lived in a tree by the front gate and who only came down once a week to dig a hole in which to wee and poo. On and on, and not even Raffy interrupted again, because the more Jack talked the more they felt like they were *there*, in another garden far away with the frogs and capybara and monkeys and giant butterflies. Raffy, sitting beside Bea on the ground, almost dared not breathe in case the sound broke the magic of Jack's storytelling. As the last traces of Leo's annoyance with his brother vanished, he put his arm around Martha. She put her head on his shoulder and sighed a little, imagining a pool fed by a waterfall. Noa, perched a little further away from the others on the steps leading up from the terrace to the meadow, pondered how she would draw Jack's garden. The nagging disappointment which had continued to dog Bea melted away.

And then . . . such a little thing.

'Sorry,' said Jack. 'I've been talking for ages. But you did ask.'

His cigarillo had gone out. Again he struck the lighter. Again, a flame shot up, illuminating his face, casting shadows. They all watched, mesmerised, as a tiny spider, drifting like a miniature parachutist on a silk thread, sailed through the circle of light.

'You should all come and visit,' Jack said. 'Alex and Ingrid had a great time when they came.'

The light went out and in they rushed, the shadows of the two people who should have been there, and the pain in Bea's chest, which she had worked so hard all afternoon to soothe, flared up again with a vengeance.

Her parents, who couldn't stick with *her* for four days, who couldn't even bring themselves to come for a *weekend*, had had a great time in Costa Rica with *Jack*?

Bea drew her knees up into her chest and wrapped her arms around them. Raffy shifted closer to her. Martha and Leo exchanged glances. Even Noa noticed. Only Jack seemed unaware as he ploughed on, making everything worse.

'They came last September for a fortnight,' he said. 'I'm surprised they didn't tell you. Ingrid kept saying how much she wished you were there.'

'Bea was at school in September,' said Leo tightly.

'Did *you* know they'd gone to Costa Rica?' Bea asked him.

'I did not,' said Leo.

Martha stood up. 'Bed, I think,' she said. 'And the kitchen to clear first.'

A bat fluttered low, drawn to the insects hovering in the faint glow of the lantern Leo had put on the table, then swerved over the steps towards the meadow, so close to Noa she felt the air displaced by its wings.

'Oh!'

'It's only a pipistrelle,' said Raffy kindly. 'It won't

hurt you. There's a whole colony of them. They live above the front door. There's a hollow behind the lintel, and a crack in the wall where they get in and out.'

'I bet she thinks bats are vampires.' Bea's words flew out, vicious, before she could stop them. 'Wait till she finds out about the toad in the bathroom! She'll probably wet her pants.'

'Bea!' said Martha sharply.

'I'm not the one who asked her here!' said Bea, and stormed into the house.

There was an embarrassed silence.

Then, '*Is* there are a toad in the bathroom?' asked Jack.

Martha stood up. 'Time for bed, you three,' she ordered the children. 'Jack and Leo can wash up.'

Up in his bedroom, Raffy changed into his pyjamas then sat on the edge of his bed in an agony of indecision.

Bea was his best friend, his chosen sister. Along with his mother, she was the person he loved most in the whole world and he would never do anything to upset her. But she *had* been rude to Noa. *Very* rude. Which wasn't fair, because poor Noa hadn't done anything wrong, and was far from home, and probably horribly lonely.

Raffy didn't like that.

Should he go and talk to Noa? Check that she was all right, apologise for Bea? And how would Bea feel, if she knew? In all his life, Raffy had never known her like this – so troubled that she was actually unkind. Would she think that he was somehow taking Noa's side against her? Would she be hurt? Would she be angry with him? That had never happened before. It wasn't a nice thought.

But he was being a coward. Raffy had read once that it took more courage to stand up to your friends than your enemies. And deep down he knew the right thing to do.

He held his breath and tiptoed to his door. Opened it, crouched to see if there was any light under Bea's.

There wasn't.

Silently, Raffy let out his breath and glided across the landing, knocked softly on Noa's door and opened it a crack.

'Can I come in?' he whispered.

Noa was sitting up in bed with her pencils and sketchbook and did not look up.

'You already have,' she said as Raffy closed the door behind him.

'What are you drawing?'

Noa didn't reply.

'I just wanted to say I'm sorry about this afternoon.' Raffy shifted uncomfortably from foot to foot. 'We shouldn't have left you at the cliff. And also, please don't be too cross with Bea. I know she was rude, but she's upset about . . .'

'Her parents, I get it,' said Noa, still not looking up.

'I just don't want you to think she's not nice,' Raffy insisted. 'Because she is. She's probably feeling terrible about how she spoke to you.'

'If you think I'm wasting my life thinking about Bea,' said Noa with almost convincing aloofness, 'then you are completely wrong. Here, you wanted to know what I was drawing.'

She held out her sketchbook. Raffy's eyes widened as he looked at her picture. It was very good. The man she had drawn was unmistakably Jack, and he was unmistakably sitting in the garden chair, and there were the lavender bushes behind him, and there was the lantern on the table, and the lighter in his right hand, and there was the tiny spider landing like a minuscule parachutist on his wrist, but why was his left hand raised like that?

'None of you saw what happened to the spider,' said Noa. 'You were all too busy listening to Jack. He squashed it, that's what he did. And what I was wondering, when you came in, was what sort of person calls hummingbirds "little flying jewels" but kills a tiny, floating spider?'

CHAPTER FOUR

C aw!

Noa hadn't expected to sleep at all, but when the raven woke her with a squawk on her first morning at Ravenwood, she struggled to remember where she was. Then the raven cawed again, and it all came flooding back.

The dragon boat, the horseshoe cove ... the flicker of a flame, the bat, Bea ...

Mum, gone.

For the whole summer.

She sat up and reached for her phone where she had put it last night, on top of her sketchbook on the chair by her bed. She had three messages.

The first was from her sister Elva.

Bonjour, pipsqueak! Pa tells me you've been exiled to the country. HOW DID THIS HAPPEN? Run away to Paris and come stay with me!

Noa's lips twitched. Elva always made her smile.

The second was from her mum, comfortingly matter-of-fact.

Just landed, darling. Tried to call last night but there was no answer. Hope that means everything is wonderful! I'll try again tomorrow xxxx

The third was from her dad. Noa opened it with trepidation.

Hope you're ok, pumpkin. Just to let you know I'm here, if ever you need/want me xxx

Noa turned on to her back and stared at the ceiling. What had she expected? For Dad to tell her he was ditching Tamsin and moving in with her?

Well, yes.

Noa closed her eyes, trying to picture Dad in the flat where she lived with Mum, sitting across from her on one of the painted chairs at the fold-down table in the kitchen.

It didn't work.

With a sigh of frustration, Noa threw off her

sheets, climbed out of bed, padded over to the window and opened the curtains.

Caw!

The raven was perched directly beneath her on the terrace, its talons gripping the back of a bench, watching her with its head on one side.

'I'm not going to try and draw you,' Noa told it. 'You'll only fly away again.'

The raven turned its back on her. Noa rolled her eyes at it and leaned on the windowsill.

The garden was in shadow, but already the air outside was warm. Doves cooed in the woods, a cuckoo gave its hooting call. Somewhere above, the trill of a robin filled the air. Higher still, she heard the eager cries of swallows and house martins already wheeling through the morning sky. And underscoring all this, in the distance, the steady murmur of the sea . . .

Noa had to admit – she might wish things were different, but it *was* lovely here.

Caw!

'All right!' Noa smiled. 'I'm coming.'

She left the window and quickly, before she

thought better of it, changed out of her nightdress into yesterday's clothes. With her shoes in her hands, she tiptoed out on to the landing. A floorboard creaked as she passed the bathroom. Noa froze.

Nothing stirred.

Holding her breath, Noa crept down the stairs and along the dark stone passage to the kitchen. The back door was unlocked. She opened it and slipped outside.

The raven, seeing her, took off and flew towards the cliff. Noa, after a split-second hesitation, ran after it.

Oh, it was a glorious morning! The sort when the world feels brand new. Noa tried to chase thoughts of her father from her mind. It was all wrong, on a morning like this, to be sad or even lonely! As she ran along the path after the raven, twisting through the meadow where already birds chattered and insects hummed, Noa remembered how it felt to be happy. The lightness of it! The sheer, light bubbliness!

The raven was waiting for her at Skidbládnir, perched at the top of the mast. As soon as she caught up, it took off again and flew out over the edge of the cliff towards the sea.

Caw!

Noa walked to the top of the path where she had stood yesterday with Bea and Raffy and looked down. The cove was completely different today, half in shadow, a crescent of gently shelving sand exposed by the low tide. The sea on the horizon was milky blue in the early light, but directly beneath Noa it was so clear she could see to the bottom.

Her heart quickened.

Careful not to slip on the dusty ground, she picked her way down the path, twisting occasionally to avoid the prickle of gorse, inhaling the scent of coconut released by a few late flowers as she brushed against them. When she reached the sand, she glanced round to check no one had followed her, then stripped down to her pants and ran to the water.

Oh, but it was cold! Like hundreds of needles made of ice. Noa paused when the water reached her mid-thighs and wrapped her arms around her shivering body.

You have to get used to the cold. That was what

Dad always said, in the days when they still went on holiday together. *Go in gradually, to let your body acclimatise, otherwise it puts too much strain on your heart.* Ah, but she didn't want to think about Dad! Not here, not now on this beautiful morning. With a cry for courage, Noa threw herself forward, gasping as the cold gripped her, and began to swim as fast as she could.

Whoosh! Whoosh! Whoosh! A strong swimmer, she soon settled into a rhythm, her body tingling, her lungs bursting, and again that bubbling joy, that lightness . . . When at last she was warm, she stopped to look behind her and saw with some surprise that she had come so far she could hardly see her pile of clothes on the beach. With a thrill of exhilaration, she turned back again to look at the open sea and saw that she was almost at the mouth of the cove.

Noa was, on the whole, sensible. She knew she should go back in, at least to where she wasn't out of her depth. But . . . it was so *big* here. So exactly the opposite of the past year spent skulking in corners of the playground and library at school, or shut in her room at the flat. Maybe she could just float a little longer, watching the ravens and gulls circle, be quiet and peaceful for a bit before ...

She sensed it before she saw it – something in the water with her, something big. Very slowly, hardly daring to look, Noa turned – there it was, just a few metres away, a mottled grey head, eyes like fathomless black marbles, huge silvery whiskers ...

A seal. A *seal*. Was it?

As panic flooded her body, Noa's brain raced. She had never seen a seal in real life before. How big were they? This one looked at least as big as her. Did they attack humans? Would this one, specifically, attack her?

Noa's eyes flicked back towards the distant shore.

There was no way she could outswim any creature that lived in the water.

The seal, apparently without moving a muscle, sank beneath the surface. Noa bit back a whimper. Animals smelled fear – she had read that in a book. But where was it? Had it gone? In ... out ... deep breaths as she looked around her. There! Far beneath her, that shadow ... Was it a rock? No, it was *moving*, cutting effortlessly towards her . . .

Noa screamed as the seal broke through the surface behind her. She thrashed around wildly, the way she used to when she first learned to swim. The creature vanished again. She felt the movement of water as it passed beneath her, resurfaced, then dived again, its body arching as it rose and fell.

Not attacking her.

Playing with her?

Noa stopped thrashing and trod water, as calmly as she could make herself. The seal resurfaced and floated, mirroring her. Noa began to swim, a measured breaststroke, her head above the surface. The seal swam too, keeping easy pace with her. Very cautiously, Noa lay on her back and gazed up at the sky, then glanced sideways. A few metres away, the seal bobbed tranquilly, its whiskery face turned towards the sun.

Panic vanished, replaced by cautious delight.

'Hello,' Noa whispered.

The seal turned its head towards her. For a few seconds, they held each other's gaze. Then the seal sank one last time. Noa waited but it did not reappear.

She let out a long breath then she swam back towards the shore, grinning from ear to ear. Her joy, however, was short-lived.

Bea and Raffy were on the beach, and they were watching her.

CHAPTER FIVE

It was the creaking floorboard that woke Bea, dragging her from sleep just long enough to tell herself Raffy or Noa had gone to the bathroom. When she woke again twenty minutes later, it was with the certain realisation that she had not heard them return.

Craning forward, Bea looked through her open door to Raffy's room. There he lay, sprawled on his back, his arms flung over his head as they always were in the morning. She crawled to the end of her bed to where she could see Noa's door.

Open, and the room empty. Where was she?

Bea slipped out of bed to the landing, glanced into the bathroom to check Noa wasn't there, then – feeling only mildly guilty – glided across to the spare room.

Who exactly was this girl Leo had foisted on them? This girl she had not been entirely fair to ...

Her first thought on entering the room was how astonishingly tidy it was. Bea's room, unless her parents were visiting, was mostly *clutter*. Noa's was the exact opposite. Her clothes were all unpacked and put away, her suitcase was stowed under the chest of drawers, the books she had brought were neatly stacked on the window seat, her nightdress was folded on her pillow. She had even made her bed.

So Noa liked order. What else could Bea learn about her? There was a phone on the chair beside the bed. Bea, who wasn't allowed a phone yet, felt a surge of envy. She picked it up but hesitated to look at the screen. Even she drew the line at going through someone's private messages. She put the phone back down and as she did her eyes fell on Noa's sketchbook.

She shouldn't. Except ... This was different from a phone – wasn't it? Pictures were *meant* to be looked at.

With a toss of her head, she picked up the sketchbook, opened it and almost immediately narrowed her eyes . . .

'What are you doing?'

Bea jumped, then squeaked with relief when she saw it was only Raffy standing in the doorway, yawning and rubbing his face.

'Look!' She held out Noa's sketchbook.

'I'm sure that's meant to be private,' said Raffy, but he edged closer. 'Are you looking at your uncle Jack and the spider?'

'What spider? No! *Look!*'

Raffy looked. 'Oh.'

'She's drawn me as a witch! And look at that raven! Circling my head like it's . . . like it's my *pet*!'

Raffy tried, not very successfully, to hide a smirk. Bea glowered at him. 'She's drawn *you* as a mouse.'

'Well, I am like a mouse in a way,' said Raffy thoughtfully.

'*How* are you like a mouse?'

'I'm small,' Raffy said. 'And I'm quite quiet. I mean, I talk a lot, but I don't shout. And I'm good at climbing trees.'

'I don't think that's why she drew you as a mouse,' growled Bea.

'Mice are cool,' Raffy insisted. 'People think they're all timid but they're actually really brave. Plus, it's a *good* mouse. Look at its ears! I think it's cute. I'm sure she didn't mean it nastily.'

'Of course she meant it nastily!' Bea hissed. 'Come on!'

She turned on her heel and went back to her room, where she threw her nightshirt on the floor and pulled on her shorts and top.

Raffy sighed and went into his own room to dress.

'Where are we going?' he asked when they met again on the landing.

'To find her,' Bea growled. 'Before she runs away or falls off the cliff or *drowns* and we get the blame. We'll try Skid first, since she was so nuts about it yesterday.'

And so to Skidbládnir they went, and not finding Noa there they looked down to the cove and saw her splashing about happily with the seal, which made Bea cross and Raffy jealous because not once in their entire life at Ravenwood had they swum with a seal, and here she was, doing it on her very first morning.

The sun was higher now, the sea glinting in the mid-morning light, the shadows on the beach all gone. It was beautiful, but the wonder of the morning was spoilt. Noa tilted her chin as she emerged from the sea, trying to look dignified despite her dripping pants. Raffy turned away to give her privacy, but Bea glared as she walked over to her clothes.

'We're not allowed to swim alone,' she said. 'It's dangerous.'

Noa finished tugging her clothes over her damp skin, then looked pointedly towards the cliffs and the ledge Bea had hurled herself from only yesterday.

Bea's lip curled. '*I* know what *I*'m doing, because *I* live here.'

Something inside Noa snapped.

'It wasn't exactly my *choice* to come here, you know!'

'It wasn't mine either,' Bea shot back. 'Especially when you think I'm a *witch*!'

Noa gasped.

Raffy, who through this exchange had been gazing thoughtfully at the sea, said, 'I have a question.'

They ignored him.

'You looked at my sketchbook!' said Noa.

'*You* drew me as a witch!'

More glaring.

'I have a *question*,' Raffy repeated.

'Oh, *what*?' Bea shouted.

'I would like to know what it was like, swimming with the seal?'

Noa wanted to be rude. She wanted to tell Raffy to go and find his own seal, if he really wanted to know, and not share hers. But there was something about the way he looked at her – patient and interested, like her answer really *mattered*.

It was a long time since Noa felt she mattered.

She hesitated, then walked around Bea to sit on the other side of Raffy on the warm damp sand, where she drew her knees up to her chin and contemplated the empty water.

'It was amazing,' she said at last. 'Like being with something ancient. Not the seal itself, I think maybe

68

from the way it was playing with me it was actually quite young, but like its *spirit* was ancient. Like it . . . like it belonged to the beginning of the world.'

She stopped, blushing, and glanced at the others from beneath downcast lashes. Had she sounded stupid? Bea's expression was unreadable, but Raffy nodded.

'Like being in a very old tree,' he said. 'Like being in Yggdrasil, and feeling you are part of something so much bigger than yourself, but still a part of it.'

'Maybe,' said Noa. 'I don't really know about trees.'

For a while, all three were quiet. Then Bea jumped to her feet. The other two watched her, a little alarmed.

'Come on, then!' she cried. 'What are you waiting for? I've got a plan.'

CHAPTER SIX

If you'd asked her, Bea might have described her change of mood as something like coming out of a fog. Yesterday she had felt lost, a confused mess of hurt and anger from which she had lashed out at Noa for the simple reason that Noa was here, and Bea's parents were not. She knew she was being unfair, but the urge to hurt someone was too strong and she couldn't stop herself. Then there had been the witch picture, and *then* her jealousy over the seal. Bea had been all set to loathe Noa when she came out of the water, but the other girl's answer to Raffy's question had been perfect.

An ancient spirit belonging to the beginning of the world.

Bea would never have thought of putting it like that, but she liked it. And so the hurt, angry, jealous fog had lifted, and Bea no longer felt lost. Quite the opposite! Now that she could see clearly, she found herself exactly where she wanted to be: at Ravenwood at the beginning of the summer holiday.

It felt good.

Plus, she had plan.

Breakfast, in Yggdrasil!

'Don't worry about the climb,' she said cheerfully to Noa, as they made their way back up the cliff. 'The rope ladder's easy once you know how. And then after breakfast we'll show you everything!'

They passed Skidbládnir, already baking in the morning sun, and followed the path back through the meadow to the terrace, where from the top of the steps, through the open kitchen door, they could see Leo and Jack talking at the kitchen table.

'I'll go in alone to get food,' decided Bea. 'It'll be quicker that way. The thing is to do it while Martha's not in the kitchen. She's pretty cool usually but sometimes she does that thing where she insists we sit down and have a proper meal at the table. Raffy, you take Noa to Ygg. I'll meet you there.'

Skipping over a startled partridge pecking at the edge of the path, she ran away towards the house. Raffy and Noa began to walk in the other direction, towards Yggdrasil.

'Why is she being so nice?' Noa asked, looking over her shoulder at Bea's retreating back.

'She *is* nice,' said Raffy. 'I told you.'

They arrived at the foot of the giant ash and looked up.

Yesterday, when she first saw the platform in Yggdrasil, Noa had thought it amazing. Now, knowing she was about to climb up to it, all she could think was how high it was, and how flimsy the rope ladder looked.

'I'll go first to show you how,' said Raffy, then skimmed up so fast Noa barely saw him touch it.

'Your turn!' he called down from the platform.

Grimly, Noa gripped the ladder with both hands. The rope was hard, smoother than she had imagined, solid but also alarmingly thin. She put her right foot on the bottom rung.

The ladder swayed.

She put her left foot on.

The ladder began to spin, knocking her against the trunk.

'I can't do it!'

'Yes, you can!' Raffy's face floated above her. Noa tried to focus on him, but her head was swimming. 'Don't grip too hard, try to breathe, and take one rung at a time. Oh, and brace your tummy muscles. That's what Leo told me to do when he put it up, and it works.'

Another deep breath. Noa raised her right foot. The ladder spun again. She whimpered but clung on. Breathed, braced. Reached higher with one hand then another, raised her left foot. Started again. Then again. And again.

'You're doing really well,' said Raffy, as she drew closer.

Noa glanced down, and shrieked.

'Don't look at the ground,' Raffy advised.

Rung by rung, Noa made it to the top of the rope ladder, where she slithered on to the platform on her belly, then crawled into the middle and stopped.

'Come to the edge,' said Raffy.

Noa groaned. Raffy crouched beside her.

'Are you scared of heights? You should have said; we could have done something else.'

'I didn't realise until today,' Noa whispered. 'I've never climbed a tree before.'

'Come anyway. I promise it's worth it. It's not dangerous or anything. All our friends come up, and no one's ever fallen off.'

They crawled together to the edge of the platform.

'Please don't do that,' Noa whimpered, as Raffy swung his legs over the side.

'What? Oh, sorry!'

He wriggled back on to the platform until he was sitting a few centimetres away from the edge. Very cautiously, Noa joined him. Raised her head. Leaned forward, mirroring Raffy . . .

and caught her breath.

The whole valley spread out before her – the track with its bordering hedgerows, the patchwork of fields, the village, the rolling hills beyond it. She looked to the right and there was the shimmering sea. Up, and there were the strong branches of the ash and glimpses of the sky.

Somewhere above she heard a tapping sound.

'Is that a woodpecker?'

'Nuthatch,' said Raffy. 'He lives here. See that hole in the trunk above us? That's his nest. Noa, do you feel it now? What you said on the beach, about being part of something old?'

Noa looked again over the valley. Everywhere, there were signs of newness – the road, the estate on the edge of the village, the fields themselves with their barbed-wire boundaries. On a distant hill, a mobile phone mast. And yet it was impossible, from up here, not to think of those other people who had stood at Ravenwood thousands of years ago, looking at those same hills and sea and coastline. Yggdrasil itself was young compared to the hills and sea, and yet ... Cautiously, Noa leaned further out to rest her hand on one of the massive boughs which supported the platform, felt the rough, tough bark under her fingers. She closed her eyes and there was something else there, something intangible but definitely present.

A spirit, perhaps.

'Yes,' she said. 'I do feel it.'

Beside her, Raffy gave a grunt of satisfaction.

Bea arrived shortly with a bulging backpack, swinging on to the platform as easily as Raffy had, and that was the end of philosophical thoughts.

'There was no need to worry about what Leo would say,' she gloated, as they spread the food out on the platform. 'He and Jack barely looked up when I went in. I basically took half the larder.'

From the rucksack she pulled three more or less squashed bananas, a punnet of strawberries, half a loaf of bread, a jar of jam, a carton of orange juice and the remains of yesterday's cake. Suddenly all starving, they ate in happy silence. But when they had finished and sat back, too full to move, Bea said brusquely to Noa:

'I'm sorry I was so horrible.'

Noa squirmed. 'I'm sorry I drew you as a witch.'

'No, I deserved it.' Bea looked at Noa earnestly. 'I was *completely* witch-like. I was just grouchy because, you know. My parents. Like one minute they're coming, then they're not, one minute they want me, then they don't. Plus they go swanning off to Costa Rica and *that* trip doesn't have to be cut short because apparently they actually *like* Uncle Jack. It's all very confusing and upsetting, not least because we would *love* to go to Costa Rica, wouldn't we, Raffy?'

'I *would*,' said Raffy cautiously. 'But not with your parents. I think that would be too stressful, even with all the wildlife.'

It was a fair point. Bea nodded, then turned back to Noa.

'Anyway,' she said. 'The point is, my parents are rubbish but if you don't mind me saying, yours don't sound great either. So …' She stuck out her hand. 'Friends?'

Noa did not reply. Her mind was reeling – partly from Bea's unexpected honesty, but mainly …

Could she be friends with Bea, after the way she had treated her yesterday?

'Please say yes,' said Raffy anxiously.

Noa swallowed.

Bea smiled tentatively. 'I promise I won't be horrible again.'

Friends. Noa's mouth began to curl. *Friends!*

She took Bea's hand and shook it.

'Phew!' Bea cried. 'For a minute there I thought you were going to refuse, and *then* what would we have done? Come on, let's make a pact. All three of us! Put your hands on mine. Come *on*! Now say after me: *I swear to make this the perfect Ravenwood summer.'*

Raffy, looking very solemn, went first. Noa followed.

'I swear . . .' she whispered.

'Louder!' said Bea.

'I SWEAR TO MAKE THIS THE PERFECT RAVENWOOD SUMMER!' Noa shouted.

As her fingers curled with Bea and Raffy's, she felt a stab of joy so deep it was almost painful.

Friends.

'We should share blood,' Raffy said. 'To make the promise stronger.'

'Ow,' said Bea.

'Spit, then.'

'Ew,' said Noa, and both girls snorted.

'I know!' Raffy jumped up and reached to pick a cluster of the ash's seeds.

'They're called keys,' he told Noa, as he distributed one each. 'To keep safe with us always, like a . . . like a talisman. Like Ygg is our witness.'

Noa looked at what he had just put in her hand. A pod, mostly flat with a bulge at the end. She held it up to the light, noticing the veins running through the translucent skin, oddly beautiful.

'Elva would like this,' she said.

'Who's Elva?' asked Raffy.

Shyly, Noa explained about her sister – Paris, the art scholarship, the polar bear picture sprayed on to a government building. 'She loves anything to do with trees and plants and animals.'

'She sounds nice,' said Raffy, very seriously.

'She is,' said Noa, with a sudden pang of sadness. 'I miss her.'

Raffy nodded. 'I would miss Bea too, if she went away.'

Bea rolled her eyes and shoved her ash key into her shorts pocket. 'No chance of *that*!' she said. 'Except for school and the dentist and things, I don't suppose I'll ever leave Ravenwood again, Come on, Noa – let's show you the rest of the place!'

*

Trouble was brewing at Ravenwood, rumbling in the background, but all through that near perfect day, Bea, Raffy and Noa were absolutely oblivious to it.

Soon after they came down from Yggdrasil, Jack went back to London.

'Something came up,' said Leo, and they did not think to question him. Why should they? There was too much to see and do to waste time thinking about the comings and goings of grown-ups.

With a last burst of willpower, Bea pushed away the confusion of her parents and threw herself into introducing Noa to Ravenwood, as generous and loud today as she had been mean and sullen yesterday, until Noa felt the loneliness of the past year melt away, replaced by a glow of happiness. Raffy, deeply relieved by the new peace, went out of his way to show her the things that Bea in her giddiness often missed. Like the entrance to a badger sett at the foot of an ancient oak, and the half-submerged frogs in the pond which, if you lay long enough among the yellow-flowered reeds on the old pontoon, you might see climb up on to lily pads to catch flies.

In the late afternoon they returned to the cove to swim, and in the early evening Martha and Leo joined them to build a fire on the rocks on which they grilled whole mackerel, then toasted slightly fishy-tasting marshmallows. The sun was quite gone by the time they left the cove. At the top of the cliff, Noa followed Bea and Raffy into Skidbládnir, where they lay on their backs to watch the stars, while Leo and Martha stood by the longboat's dragon head, talking in low voices as they watched the waning moon.

'I love it here so much,' Leo said.

'I know,' Martha replied. 'I know.'

The children did not question the note of sadness in Leo's voice any more than they had questioned Jack's leaving.

By the time she climbed into bed, Noa felt she had known Ravenwood all her life. She picked up her phone and there was a message from Mum:

> Sweet one, send news? How is
> everything? Are they looking after
> you? xxx

Noa, thinking of all she had done in just one day – the seal! Climbing Yggdrasil, discovering she had vertigo, conquering vertigo! The barbecue, the pond, two new friends! – replied with three kisses as Bea, spluttering toothpaste around the washbasin, called out her plans for tomorrow from the bathroom – get started on the tree house! Find the seal! Walk round the headland at low tide to the next cove!

'Look for the newt!' called Raffy from his bedroom.

'*Not* look for the newt,' yelled Bea, with a scream of laughter.

They talked on late into the night through the open doors of their bedrooms, until the air cooled and one by one they fell asleep, hugging their promise close.

A perfect Ravenwood summer.

They did not think, any of them, how often promises are broken.

CHAPTER SEVEN

The call that would change everything came the next morning shortly after ten o'clock, when they were all in the kitchen, just back from a swim. Leo was making coffee, Martha sorting laundry, Raffy and Noa were laying the table. Bea sat on the countertop, barefoot and skin sticky with salt, holding forth about a new plan which had just this minute occurred to her – to gather all the recycling and, by means as yet undecided, turn it into a sculpture of a seal.

'Or maybe a dolphin,' she said, waving a piece of toast. 'A seal would be more *here*, but dolphins are prettier. I'm sorry, they just are. And when we've finished, we can get Noa's sister to put it on Instagram.'

Noa, enjoying herself hugely, poured more cornflakes into a bowl. 'Why Elva?' she asked.

Bea rolled her eyes. 'Because it's a protest, obviously! Against all the rubbish in the sea. You know, that gets eaten by fish.'

And then, before Raffy could say, 'Dolphins aren't fish they're mammals,' the house phone rang in the hall and Leo said, 'Get that will you, Bea? Your Instagram dolphin is making my head hurt,' and Bea skipped out to answer, and it was Alex.

When the call was over, she carried the phone back to the kitchen, laid it on the table, sat down and stared at it as if it might explode.

Then she told them.

Alex and Ingrid had arrived in Venice. Tomorrow evening, they were going to take a ferry across the Adriatic Sea to Croatia to pick up a sailing yacht, which they were going to sail along the coast all the way back to Venice. After that they were going to stay in a friend's villa, where there would be a swimming pool and olive groves and from which they could go and visit beautiful cultural places. They wanted Bea to fly out and join them.

A wave of shock swept around the kitchen.

'When?' demanded Leo.

'Tomorrow.'

'*Tomorrow?*'

'You're not going, though,' said Raffy. 'You *can't* go. You *said* – the day before yesterday, in Ygg, you *said* if they asked, you wouldn't go.'

But even as he spoke an awful panic began to steal over him. Bea *was* thinking about it – she was definitely thinking about it. And it was stupid! It would end badly, and she would cry again, and he . . .

Raffy's eyes prickled.

He would miss her *so much*.

'You don't have to go just because they ask you,' he said, hating that he sounded so whiny. 'You can say no.'

'Raffy, love,' said Martha.

'It's true!' he insisted, wishing that his voice hadn't begun to shake. 'Look at Noa! Everyone wanted *her* to go and stay with her dad, but she didn't! She came here instead. Tell her, Noa!'

Noa stared at her cereal. Raffy scowled.

'Tell her!'

But all Noa could think of was yesterday and the promise they had made together in Yggdrasil, that stab of joy because at last she had made friends again.

What did it mean though, to be friends? Did friends tell each other the truth? *Look at Noa*, Raffy had said, but she had no idea what Bea should do. All she knew was that when it came to tricky parents, there were no easy answers.

'I think probably Bea needs to decide what she wants,' she stammered, as Raffy pressed her again. 'I mean, she has to decide what's right for her.'

Raffy made a sound like steam escaping from a kettle.

Martha sat down beside Bea. 'What do you want to do?' she asked.

'I don't know.'

Bea looked up from the phone at the others. Leo was frowning, leaning against the counter with his hands around his coffee mug. On the bench, on the far side of the table, Raffy was looking mutinous. Beside him, Noa pushed cornflakes around her bowl.

Oh, this was impossible!

'What do *you* all think I should do?'

Noa shook her head, like she had nothing more to add.

Raffy stuck his chin out and said, 'I think you shouldn't go.'

Leo grunted. 'On the basis of the last trip, I have to say I agree.'

Martha frowned at him, then put one hand over Bea's and said, 'Noa's right. It's your choice, and we will support whatever decision you make.'

Alone at Skidbládnir, Bea sat with her back against the hull to think.

On the one hand, there was Ravenwood. The cove, the cliffs, Ygg, the long easy summer stretching ahead. She was so safe here, so happy! On the other hand ... there might be hurt, certainly, but also – oh, also there might be stories and cuddles and that strange, fairy-tale feeling of discovering that her parents loved her. The trip to France had unlocked something in her, like a door into her heart, feelings she had never known she had. She couldn't just close that door again, even if she wanted to. She pressed her head into Skidbládnir's folded dragon wing.

'What do *you* think I should do?'

Somewhere in the sky above, like a message from a witch or a god willing her to be brave, she heard a raven call.

The next morning, standing by the van in the relative cool of dawn, Bea almost changed her mind.

Martha came out to see her off, wrapped in her old cotton dressing gown, and Noa in startlingly uncreased pink pyjamas, but Raffy did not leave his room.

'He's just sad you're going,' said Martha.

Bea's lower lip trembled. Raffy had barely spoken to her yesterday, but stayed out in the woods while Martha and Noa helped her pack. Then last night, when everyone else was in bed and she had gone into his room to try to explain why she was going, he hadn't wanted to listen. Had, in fact, told her she was being stupid.

Was she, though? Her decision had seemed right to her when she made it, but now she wasn't sure. She tried to remember her reasoning – something to do with a raven, with doors opening and fairy tales. In the light of morning, as Leo put a small red suitcase into the van, it all felt a bit confusing.

'I don't want Raffy to be sad,' she whispered. 'Maybe I shouldn't go.'

Martha took Bea's chin in her hand.

'You listen to me, Beatrice Pembury,' she said. 'I have *been* to Venice, and it's amazing. As is Croatia. You are going to see the world and you are going to have a wonderful time. You leave Raffy to us. We'll look after him.'

'But what if my parents . . .'

Martha, who had spent half the night worrying about a repeat of the French holiday disaster, pulled Bea into a hug.

'Your parents love you very much,' she said, trying hard to believe what she was saying. 'They wouldn't have invited you if they didn't. This is exactly what you need, to spend some time together. And we'll all be here when you get back.'

Bea gulped, but nodded. When Martha let her go, she turned to Noa.

'Thank you for getting up to say goodbye,' she said. 'I'm sorry I'm leaving when we've just made friends.'

Noa blushed. She almost hadn't come out this morning, in case people thought she was intruding on a family farewell, but she had something important to do.

'I made this for you.' From the pocket of her pyjamas, she pulled a small piece of sketching paper, folded in two like a card. Bea opened it and gasped. On the inside of the card, life-size and delicate, Noa had drawn a perfect copy of an ash key.

'It's just to wish you a good holiday,' Noa stammered. 'And to say, I'll be here too when you get back.'

'I love it,' said Bea, and meant it. The picture and the thought behind it had given her new heart. She gave Noa a quick hug. 'When I get back,' she whispered, 'we will have the absolute *best* time. I promise.'

'Come on.' Leo – who had spent half the night wondering how he could persuade Bea to change her mind – bowed now to the inevitable. 'We'd better get going, or you're going to miss that flight.'

*

They drove for the most part without talking, listening to the radio. Bea slipped Noa's card into the backpack on her knees, keeping it close, but the further they went from home, the more she felt the courage it had given her seep away. Mouth dry, ears ringing, insides squeezed by invisible hands, she felt just as she had two days ago, standing on the high ledge about to jump, except now there was no sparkling sea waiting to receive her, no warm sunshine on her face – just a long plane trip in the care of strangers and, waiting at the end, the uncertainty of her parents' reaction.

Was it really worth putting herself through this?

When they turned off the motorway to the airport, she finally spoke.

'Do you think Raffy will ever forgive me?'

'Course he will.' Leo shot her sideways smile. 'He loves you.'

'Do you always forgive people you love?'

'Always!' said Leo. 'Well, mostly. But Raffy definitely will.'

He parked in the multi-storey short-term car park but didn't get out of the van. Instead, he opened the glove compartment and pulled out a small, padded envelope.

'It's an old phone of mine,' he said, as Bea opened it. 'I know we said no phones until you start at Meadowbanks in September, but I thought in the circumstances it was a good idea. There wasn't time to get a new one, but it works, and the camera isn't bad. There's a charger in there too, and a European adaptor plug, and I've put in my number and Martha's, and also Noa's – I thought you might send her a message. It *is* a bit rough on her, you going away when you've only just made friends. Oh, and I've put a tracker on it, in case anything happens. I was going to give it to you last night but I didn't want to make Raffy jealous, when he's already so upset.'

He grinned as he handed her the envelope.

'I have to say I am rather impressed with myself for remembering I still had this. And for finding the right charger. Martha couldn't believe it.'

Only yesterday, getting her own phone would have sent Bea into giddy ecstasy, but today it just reminded her of how far away she was going. She took the envelope and peered inside suspiciously.

'Thank you,' she said. 'What do you mean, *in case anything happens*?'

Leo shrugged. 'I don't know. In case you got lost or something.'

Bea swallowed. Getting lost on the continent of Europe was not something she had thought about.

'What happens if I get lost but I don't *have* my phone?' she asked. 'What if somebody steals it? What if I get *kidnapped*?'

'Then I'll call the police,' said Leo. 'And I won't rest until I've found you. Come on, put the phone away and let's go and check in. I wish I'd never mentioned the tracker. Everything is going to be fine.'

In a windowless room at the end of the check-in concourse, Bea waited on a plastic chair beside a boy with dark skin and bright yellow hair, as Leo and a flight attendant called Habiba went through paperwork.

Paperwork to prove Bea was who Leo said she was. That Leo was who he said *he* was. That Alex and Ingrid were who Leo said they were, and that they would be at the airport to meet Bea when Leo said they would, where they would produce papers to prove they were who *they* said they were.

'It's like we're parcels,' the yellow-haired boy whispered.

Bea stared at him.

'Like we're being posted and have to be signed for,' he explained. 'Is this the first time you fly alone? Don't be scared. I do it all the time.'

'I'm not scared,' Bea lied.

'Good!' said the boy. 'Because you absolutely shouldn't be. I'm Josh, by the way.'

The paperwork finished, Bea's suitcase was checked in and they all walked through the airport together towards the departure gate. All the while, Josh counted off the places he had flown to.

'Just in the last year I went to New York at Easter, Geneva in February, Goa at Christmas, Barcelona for November half-term...'

I might hit him, thought Bea.

At passport control, Leo hugged her goodbye.

'You can come home whenever you want.' His voice broke a little as he whispered in her ear. 'If you miss us too much, or if ... well, you know.

Absolutely whenever you want.'

Bea hugged him back, unable to speak. For a few wild seconds, she considered begging him to take her home with him. But then he let her go, and Habiba began to usher her and Josh towards the passport desk. Bea turned for one last wave, but Leo was already walking away. She felt suddenly very small and alone.

'In *June* half-term there was Rome,' said Josh. 'And Mauritius last summer, which makes six. Twelve if you count there and back. My parents adore travelling. It's their passion.'

I will *hit him*, thought Bea.

There was a brief respite while they went separately through the security scanner, then Josh joined her on the bench where she was putting her shoes back on, words pouring out of his mouth with no evident control.

'They don't even wait for school holidays,' he burbled. 'They just fly off while I'm at boarding school, and when term ends my godmother pops me on a plane. We're actually going to stay in her villa now near Venice. She's lending it to us. What are you doing?'

'We're going sailing.'

'Oh, I like sailing. To be honest, I don't know how long we're going to stay at the villa. My parents get bored *very* quickly. Once – it's quite funny really – we left Paris right in the middle of dinner. Mum just said, shall we go to Italy? And off we went ...'

They'll be at the cove now at home, thought Bea, with a tug of longing.

At the departure gate, through a glass wall, she saw a buggy piled with bags driving towards a plane and thought she glimpsed her own red suitcase somewhere in the middle. This was it, then. She was really going – leaving Ravenwood, Raffy, everything she loved, flying off towards the unknown ... *Only for two weeks*, she reminded herself, but her breath came short and shallow as she followed Josh and Habiba down a flight of stairs and out on to the tarmac to join the queue of passengers shuffling towards a ramp of steps up to the plane.

'I can't do it.'

With no warning, Josh stopped. Behind them, people bumped into each other. Somebody swore.

'Can't do what, dear?' asked Habiba.

'Fly,' said Josh. 'I'm too scared.'

Bea gaped at him. 'But you've flown loads of times! Twelve times already this year, if you count there and back. If *you're* scared, what should I be?'

Grumbling passengers began to flow around them. Josh didn't budge.

'Just because I fly a lot doesn't mean I like it. Flying's mad. It makes no sense. Planes are like a giant metal birds.'

'Giant metal birds, indeed!' said Habiba, with somewhat strained cheerfulness. 'Come on, the pair of you!'

Josh ignored her.

'I begged and begged to be allowed to take the train. You can get from London to Venice in twenty-four hours. I know it's long, but I don't care. There's a night train from Paris, and they have beds! The train goes through mountains. I like mountains. They're solid.'

Josh began to cry. Bea's insides were so twisted now they felt like a solid hard lump, but it helped a little to see that he was even more scared than her.

'We'll do it together.' She reached for his hand. It was clammy, but she held it anyway. 'Come on! I'll tell you a story.'

All the way up the steps, then as they strapped themselves into their seats and waited for take-off, Bea told Josh about Ravenwood. As she spoke, she forgot to be scared herself. The smell of kerosene, the piped music in the cabin, the strangers jostling past with bags and cases, all faded into the background. Just talking about home made her feel better.

The engines revved. Josh grabbed Bea's hand again.

'Tell me more about the bats,' he said. 'Do they really live inside the house?'

The plane wobbled towards the runway, the engines grew louder. Everything shook, the world outside sped past, the plane lifted. They were up and they were off and everything familiar was left behind.

Far below, in the wood-panelled study of an expensive London flat, Jack Pembury stood at an antique desk with another man, scrolling through photographs on a tablet.

'What do you think?' asked Jack.

The man grunted. 'You're sure he'll agree?'

'He'll have to. We won't leave him a choice.'

CHAPTER EIGHT

Raffy was awake when Bea left. Through his open window he listened to the crunch of shoes on the gravel path, the low murmur of voices. When he heard the doors of the van slam shut and Martha and Noa calling goodbye, he balled his fists, fighting the urge to run out. Even if he did catch up with Bea, what would he say? Beg her not to go? He had already done that last night. Wish her well on her travels? He was too angry with her. How *could* Bea leave? After last time, and yesterday, and the pact they had made?

The van's engine started, grew louder then fainter as it drove away, there was the crunch of footsteps again as Martha and Noa returned to the house. Raffy felt an urgent need to be outside, but he couldn't bear the thought of other people. He waited until he was sure Martha and Noa weren't coming upstairs. When he heard them go into the kitchen, he tiptoed out of his room, then ran quietly down to the hall and out of the front door.

Where should he go?

Not the cove or Skidbládnir – Martha was bound to go for a swim soon, and he didn't want her to find him. And Ygg was too full of yesterday's broken promise . . .

The woods, then, the cool green woods which always made everything better. Raffy set off at a run across the meadow, his bare feet thumping on the dry cracked earth. He slowed to a walk when he reached the trees, waiting for them to weave their usual magic, but his mind would not keep still.

The pond was in full shade at this time of day, almost black, its reflections sharp and clear. Raffy lay on the old pontoon and, with a stick, drew circles in the water.

A fairy pool, Bea called the pond when it was like this. She claimed it showed you exactly what you wanted, swore her reflection in it had fewer freckles and straighter hair. Ignoring the creaks of the rotting wood beneath him, Raffy leaned over until his face hovered just above the surface, but his reflection showed him nothing different from what he saw in the bathroom mirror – a small brown boy with round cheeks and a slight bump in his nose from where he had broken it falling out of a tree when he was six years old.

What *did* he want?

Something in the water moved, close to the surface. Raffy caught his breath. For a fleeting moment, he stopped thinking about Bea. Could this be ...?

No, it couldn't. Newts were nocturnal and anyway, this late in the year they should be living on dry land. But everything was different with the heatwave. The leaves on the trees were already turning, flowers were wilting early and yesterday – only yesterday! – when they showed Noa the pond, Raffy had noticed a female mallard on her third clutch of eggs this year. So *maybe* ...

The something dived, then resurfaced by a lily pad. Raffy let out a disappointed sigh and rolled on to his back, dropping the stick on the pontoon. He was fond of frogs, but at Ravenwood they weren't exactly rare.

What did he want?

Through a gap in the trees, high in the impossibly blue sky, he watched an aeroplane pass. That would be Bea soon, flying off to Italy for her perfect holiday with her parents. In his mind, he replayed their argument last night. After he had begged her to stay, Bea had said, in a little voice he hated because it didn't sound like her, 'I just want to make everything better.'

'How?' Raffy had spat. 'You are literally making everything worse!'

'What happened in France,' she had replied, almost inaudible, and that was when he had whisper-shouted at her that she was being stupid, she hadn't done anything wrong in France, it was her parents' fault the holiday had ended the way it did.

A new feeling began to steal through Raffy's body as he suddenly understood something, icy as the pond's dark waters.

He wasn't just hurt, he was afraid.

Bea had *always* tried to make things better with her parents, only he was so used to it he had never realised. The Christmas presents she pretended to like, the way she tidied whenever they came, the way she went so quiet in front of them, as though her usual loudness might offend them ...

Once, years ago, after one of Alex and Ingrid's visits, Raffy had asked Martha why he didn't have any family. He knew his father had gone away before he was born, but wasn't there anyone else – uncles, aunts, grandparents? Martha had looked so sad he never asked her again. But then she had held him tight and said, 'You do have family, love. You and me and Leo and Bea, we are exactly like a family, aren't we? We'll always have each other.' He had accepted this, and he thought Bea had too, but things were changing. Now, twice in one year, Alex and Ingrid had taken Bea away.

We'll always have each other, Martha had said, but families split up. Look at Noa! Her dad living with his girlfriend and her twins, her mother doctoring far away, her sister in Paris ... Look what had happened to her – sent away to live with strangers!

Raffy pressed his fingers into the splintered wood of the pontoon as terrifying questions tumbled through his mind.

What was it Bea had said, when her parents brought her back early from France?

Why didn't they keep me?

He had thought at the time that she was talking about their holiday, but what if it went back further than that – all the way to the beginning, when Bea was a baby?

And what if this time Bea's parents decided they *did* want to keep her?

What would Bea do then?

That same afternoon, after Leo returned from the airport, Nick came up from the village to start work on the tree house. Over the following days, in sweltering heat, Raffy, Leo and Noa helped him build it, exactly as Raffy had described to Bea, a little cabin with a pitched roof and a window over the valley, with four bunks inside, which opened to store blankets and pillows, shelves for books, the pulley system.

Nick was a good teacher, gentle and kind, and his passion for working with wood was infectious. Very soon, as the tree house began to take shape, a merry camaraderie developed between the workers. Leo, always in his element working with his hands, seemed to grow more carefree with each passing hour, until by the end of the second day he was singing an impressive repertoire of old musical numbers, and making his co-workers join in the chorus. Nick responded by teaching them old folk songs he had learned from his grandfather. Even Martha got involved. She had announced at the beginning of the project that she would be spending this first week of the holidays reading in the shade. But when the singing started, tree-house fever gripped her too, and on the third day she got out an old sewing machine, cut up an old yellow bedspread and turned it into cushion covers for the bunks, laughing when Leo used them as props, wearing them as hats or cloaks to accompany his songs.

For Noa, it was a happy time, calm but busy. It was comforting, after the past year, to be with grown-ups who all got on so well, and it was exciting to be part of something, to feel valued and like she belonged. But her crowning pleasure were the daily messages she, along with Leo and Martha, was receiving from Bea.

Bea, clearly reconciled to her new phone, sent a *lot* of messages.

Pictures – so many pictures! Of Bea in a stone street in blazing summer light, wearing sunglasses and a new green dress, of the sailing yacht, which was called the *Carolina*, small and sleek with white sails and a blue hull, of pizzas, peaches on a market stall, Ingrid and Alex eating ice cream with their feet hanging over a harbour quay. And captions – so many captions! Usually in the form of hashtags – #shopping, #pleasecanwegetaboat? #yummy.

There were proper messages too, short but numerous.

My cabin is so tiny! I love it! I'm basically sleeping in a cupboard!

Yesterday I ate pasta with truffles and it was the most delicious thing I ever tasted!

Noa responded with pictures of her own – of

the evolving tree house, of sunset over the cove, of a robin pecking at crumbs from her lunchtime sandwich. Every time Bea responded – with a heart, or a kiss, or yet another picture – Noa's heart gave a little flip, because friends at a distance was still friends.

Her only sadness was the slight coolness which seemed to have developed between her and Raffy. Being Raffy, he was never anything but polite to her, but there was a distance between them now that hadn't been there before. She thought at first that he blamed her for not trying to stop Bea from leaving. But when she had tried to apologise, he looked astonished and said he had forgotten about that. Possibly, she thought, he was just missing Bea. Or he was jealous because, not having a phone, he wasn't getting the messages directly. Whatever the reason, she was sorry they weren't closer.

Raffy, in fact, was in turmoil. He had looked forward so much to building the tree house! He worked hard, and tried to join in with the merriment, even the singing, but the thoughts which had so terrified him in the woods wouldn't leave him alone, and his heart wasn't in it.

Bea's messages! There was something not quite right about them, in Raffy's opinion. 'She's happy,' Martha had said, when they started to arrive, and, 'Thank God for that!' Leo had agreed. Neither of them was paying enough attention.

Bea *hated* shopping. And dresses. And she *never* used words like *yummy*.

She was trying too hard, thought Raffy. Doing everything right to please her parents.

And where, oh where, would that lead to?

When, oh when, would it stop?

Five days after Bea's departure, Nick, Leo, Raffy and Noa crowded on to the platform to admire their work. To mark the occasion, Leo produced a red ribbon from the pocket of his work trousers, which he tied across the cabin door.

'Back in five minutes!' he said and scrambled down the rope ladder.

He returned with Martha, who cut the ribbon with great ceremony.

'I do declare this tree house OPEN!' she said. 'And I have brought gifts!'

'Behold!' said Leo, stepping across the platform to the pulley. 'Here comes the first bucket! And *not* the one for weeing in!'

The gifts which duly appeared in the non-wee bucket were a cake tin (complete with cake), plates and a set of mugs no longer needed in the house, a thermos flask and an old tablecloth which they spread over the floor of the cabin for a picnic.

It was a jolly party. Martha praised the bunks, the pulley system, the shelves, the view from the window. Nick, though a man of few words, gave an emotional speech about how happy it made him to have given new shape to the fallen beech tree whose wood they had used. Leo wondered whether they should go into business making tree houses.

'Especially with our two budding carpenters here,' he said, beaming at Raffy and Noa.

Noa blushed with pleasure. Raffy, troubled by Bea's latest message describing the super scrummy clams she had eaten for lunch – *super scrummy?* And she hated shellfish! – tried to smile back.

'Let's take a photo to send to Bea!' Leo said now, whipping out his phone. 'Everyone squeeze together and say *tree house*!'

In the picture, Raffy was the only one not grinning.

'Love, are you sure you're all right?' Martha asked later, when they had come down from Yggdrasil and were walking together back towards the house. 'You've been so quiet lately. I know you're missing Bea, we all are, but is there something else?'

He hadn't wanted to say anything until now, in case it made his fear too real, but it was hard not to answer direct questions from his mum.

'All her messages,' he said. 'Peaches and truffles and clams. Don't you think they're a bit ... much?'

'It's good Bea's happy with her parents,' said Martha gently.

'But what if ...'

What if Bea's parents decided to keep her?

What would she do then?

He couldn't say it out loud. 'It doesn't matter.'

Martha kissed the top of his head. 'Come for a swim with Noa and me?'

Raffy shook his head. 'I'm going to get some books to take up to the tree house,' he said.

Upstairs, Raffy didn't look for books, but lay on Bea's bed and stared at the reflective stars which covered the ceiling. Leo had put them up for her seventh birthday. Raffy remembered it perfectly. It had taken hours, as Bea decided exactly where she wanted each star to go, not in the shape of the galaxy but of a giant sunflower.

When they slept out in the tree house, they could look at real stars . . .

He turned on to his side and laid his hand on Bea's pillow, thinking of Leo's stories, how he always described the way they had held hands on that first drive up to Ravenwood, and how Martha said they had never really let go.

And now a new question began to form . . .

The question was short and it was simple but it was eleven years in the making. Once it got its hooks into him, it would not let him go.

Change happens slowly at first, they say, then speeds up until it's very fast.

That evening, just as the inhabitants of Ravenwood were sitting down to dinner, Jack returned to Ravenwood. This time, he brought a friend.

CHAPTER NINE

Jack's friend Anthony 'Ant' Rainer had been at school with Jack and had come to Ravenwood a lot in his teens. Loud, shiny and unmissable in a fuchsia polo shirt and deep orange suntan, he glided up the track with Jack at his side in a gleaming SUV and blustered into their lives as if he had never left.

He was, at first, exactly what they all needed.

Ever since Nick had gone back down to the village, the excitement of finishing the tree house had abated. Leo, Martha and Noa, flushed with the satisfaction of a job well done, had been buoyant enough as they sat down to dinner. But Raffy, still gripped by the momentous question formed as he lay on Bea's bed, sat before his plate unable to speak, and his silence weighed on them. If Bea had been there, she would have roused them with a new plan for tomorrow. Since she wasn't, the mood around the table grew steadily more and more glum. In the circumstances, Ant was – at first – exactly what they needed.

'I'm sorry to arrive unannounced,' he said to Martha. 'Jack said it would be OK, and I'm so glad to be here! Stick me anywhere – in a shed, if you have to! Or in that excellent tree house I saw driving in. People pay good money to sleep in tree houses, you know. Food! I'm starving! God that looks good! Is there enough for me? I warn you, I eat a *lot*!'

It was impossible to resist such enthusiasm. With a friendly laugh, Martha dismissed the notion there might not be enough to eat and told Raffy to lay another two places at the table. Leo, initially disconcerted by the sudden arrival, opened a bottle of wine. Even Raffy, despite his gloom, smiled at the idea of Ant trying to bed down in one of the tree house's narrow bunks. Noa, relieved by the change of atmosphere, amused herself drawing Ant in her mind, first as a big cat, then a bright-eyed eagle, then – as he did indeed eat a lot – a rippling boa constrictor.

Everything about Ravenwood was wonderful, said Ant, tucking into tomato pasta. The food! The wine! Martha showed him up to Alex's room and it was splendid – not as fun as a tree house, to be sure, but definitely more comfortable! What a view from the window! The house, with its threadbare carpets and faded furnishings looked somewhat shabby compared to his general glossiness, but he didn't seem to notice. *Everything* was splendid!

The blow, when it came, was couched in pleasantries.

After dinner, they wandered together to watch the sunset from Skidbládnir, and again Ant thought everything was perfect. The meadow! The flowers! The sheer wonder of the Viking longboat against the pink and purple sky! How had Leo made it? From a fallen tree! Incredible – what vision Leo had! How clever he was! The tree had fallen the night before Martha and Raffy came, and Bea? What a story! How long ago was that, exactly? Eleven years! And where, Ant asked Martha, did her family live?

'All my family are here,' said Martha.

It was what she always said, when people asked. And maybe if Raffy's mind hadn't already been full of questions, if he hadn't lain on Bea's bed earlier thinking about that day eleven years ago when he and Martha first came to Ravenwood, if Leo hadn't just told the story again … maybe then he wouldn't have paid such close attention to Martha's reaction, noticed the fraction of a pause before her reply, her forced stillness, or the brightness with which she immediately said there was still a bit of daylight left, didn't Ant and Jack want a swim? It would be so nice after their long drive, especially as the night was so warm.

But all these things had happened. Raffy *had* lain on Bea's bed, and he *had* thought about that day. It was glaringly obvious to him that Martha was avoiding Ant's question. Surely other people must have noticed? He glanced at Leo. His expression was unreadable.

A swim, Ant cried, was exactly what he needed! A skinny dip in the cove as the moon came up, just like he and Jack used to do as boys! And away he galloped down the cliff path, Jack following close behind.

Everything went very quiet.

'Let's go and clear up the kitchen,' said Leo, but neither Raffy nor Martha moved.

'Come on, Noa,' said Leo, and she must have sensed something too, because as she left she cast a curious glance back over her shoulder.

When the others were gone, mother and son continued to sit opposite each other in Skidbládnir, watching a charm of goldfinches on a patch of purple teasel sing to the setting sun.

'I came here on my very first morning,' said Martha when the birds took off again, spooked by a circling sparrowhawk. 'There was no Skidbládnir in those days of course, and hardly even any goldfinches. Just mess everywhere because of the storm, but even then I knew the place was special.'

'Mum.'

Raffy thought he saw her hands shake before she folded them in her lap. Perhaps he shouldn't do what he was about to do, he thought. Perhaps he and Martha should get up now and follow Leo and Noa back to the kitchen, pretending they didn't both know what he was about to ask.

But it was too late. When an eleven year old question wakes up, you can't ignore it and hope it goes away.

'Mum,' Raffy said. 'Why did we come to Ravenwood?'

Long after everyone had gone to bed, Noa sat by her window. Brow furrowed, jaw clenched, ivy curling over her shoulder through the open casement, she sat with her sketchbook on her knees, drawing a dragon. She couldn't sleep.

First Bea had left, now Raffy was going too – to London, tomorrow morning, with Martha. Leo was driving them to the station. She had heard him and Martha arguing about it on the terrace earlier, when they didn't know she was listening. Leo had begged Martha to stay.

I need you here, he had said. *At least wait until Jack has left ...*

I've waited long enough, Martha had replied before adding, mysteriously, *I always promised myself that when Raffy asked me I would tell him.*

Then, as if Raffy and Martha leaving weren't bad enough:

What about Noa? Leo had cried. *What am I going to do with her with everyone gone?*

You invited her, Martha had replied. *You think of something.*

The words swam round Noa's mind as she drew. What a fool she had been, ever to think she belonged here!

She finished her drawing and held it up to the light. Her dragon was calm, almost serene, floating with open wings through a summer sky. A good dragon, but wrong. Noa reached for her pencil case and took out an eraser, rubbed away the long neck stretched towards the sun and redrew it in an angry curve. Widened the nostrils to a flare. Closed the eyes to narrow slits. Drew talons, curved and cruel, like weapons of war. Curled back the lips and spat out a plume of smoke and flames.

What am I going to do with Noa?

You invited her.

Martha and Leo would have been appalled, had they known those careless words, thrown out in confusion and ill temper, had found their way to Noa's ears. But found their way they had, and wormed their way into her heart.

And careless words have consequences.

PART TWO

CHAPTER TEN

From the moment their train started to pull through the suburbs, with every cell in his body, Raffy hated London.

Hated the rows of identical houses in rows of identical streets. The baffling advertising hoardings, the cranes that pierced the skyline, the city's overwhelming grubbiness. Any greenery he saw was trapped, concreted into pavements or imprisoned behind railings. His heart lifted briefly when the train ran alongside a park, then sank again when he saw how far from each other the trees were planted, with none of the tangled undergrowth of a natural wood.

He already missed home.

At Liverpool Street, a wave of other passengers swept them along the platform, and Raffy felt like he was drowning with nothing to cling to. Even Martha was little comfort to him, rushing like everyone else, as different here from the mother he knew at Ravenwood as the London parks were from the woods of home; sharper, quicker, her body more tense, her eyes more alert as she strode across the concourse and down the steps to the Underground. She had not yet told him what they were doing here. Yesterday in Skidbládnir, after he had asked his question, she had gone very quiet, the way she did sometimes, deep inside herself to think, and then she had said she needed to make a phone call, and after she had made the phone call she had asked, how would Raffy feel about a trip to London the very next day? To which a stunned Raffy had stammered, 'OK, I guess, but why?'

'I'll explain when we get there,' Martha had said, after another long pause.

As yet, there had been no explanation.

In the Underground station, Martha bought two tickets from a machine then marched towards the escalators, with Raffy scurrying to keep up. Their train arrived almost immediately, screeching to a halt alongside the grimy platform. The doors opened and a stream of passengers poured out. An even larger stream poured in, Raffy and Martha among them. Raffy found himself standing with his face in a stranger's armpit, trying not to breathe, while beside him Martha, the most patient person he knew, tapped her fingers on the handrail and counted off the stops under her breath.

They came out of the station on to a busy avenue on a steep hill, baking in the midday sun.

'This way,' said Martha, and set off up the hill.

Raffy ran after her, trying not to stumble as he took in their surroundings.

People, people, people, all moving … A man with grey dreadlocks on an old bicycle with a ladder hitched over his shoulder, a couple squeezed together on an electric scooter, a courier weaving in and out of traffic on a motorbike, an old lady with clothbound feet pushing a shopping trolley full of plastic bags. Women with prams, tourists with maps, people on lunch breaks with packets of sandwiches, people in suits on mobile phones ... And shops! So many shops! Bakeries, florists, newsagents. Coffee shops, betting shops, vaping shops, all crammed in next to each other along the hot, litter-strewn pavement ...

'Come *on*, Raffy!'

He realised he had slowed down, and sped up again.

After a few blocks, the shops gave way to large houses and the road grew quieter, shaded by towering plane trees. Raffy stopped to catch his breath by the first one they came to, feeling a pang of sadness at its tar-smothered roots. Instinctively, he laid his hand on the mottled grey trunk and looked up into the branches.

A red-ringed eye in a bright green face peered back.

'Mum, there's a *parrot*!'

Martha stopped reluctantly and looked up, then gave a faint smile.

'It's a parakeet,' she said. 'There are lots. They shouldn't be here, really. They used to be kept as pets, but people let them go years ago. There was some sort of health scare, rumours they spread disease. Now the city is full of them.'

'I didn't know.' Raffy gazed at the parakeet in wonder.

'Evolution, I suppose.' Martha squeezed his shoulder. 'Who needs Costa Rica, eh? Come on, we'll be late.'

Left down a side street, right, left again. The houses were smaller here than on the avenue. Raffy had lost all sense of direction, but Martha kept going, pausing only very briefly now and then to check her bearings, until at last, halfway down a tree-lined street, she stopped before a metal gate.

'This is it.'

Raffy barely had time to take in his surroundings – a bed of lavender and some tall pink hollyhocks, a tiled path, a two-storey house built of red brick – when the front door flew open and a woman stepped out.

Raffy stared.

The woman was tiny, but stood very straight and poised. She was dressed in an old-fashioned blue-flowered dress, the long braids pulled back in a bun were grey and she wore thick glasses, but there was no mistaking who she looked like.

'There you are at last!' said the woman.

Martha took a deep breath.

'Raffy,' she said. 'Meet Grandma.'

CHAPTER ELEVEN

The street, the hollyhocks, the two women, the house, all disappeared. Raffy stood stock-still by the metal gate with his mouth wide open.

He had a grandmother?

'Come along, come along!' Grandma, evidently, was just as brisk as Martha, though the small hands in Raffy's back as she began to usher him along the path were a lot sharper. 'Let's get you inside!'

Raffy, flustered, glanced back at Martha, who scrunched up her face, part hopeful, part apologetic.

And well might she be apologetic, Raffy thought indignantly. How had she never told him he had a *grandmother*?

At the threshold of the house, he paused. A heavy

curtain hung across the inside of the front door. Grandma did not open it, but lifted a corner and slipped behind it, then held it up for Raffy to follow.

'In you come then, Rafael!'

He stepped inside and gulped as Grandma dropped the curtain.

It took a few seconds for Raffy's eyes to adjust to the darkness. When they did, despite the heat of the day, he shivered. He was in a long, gloomy hallway, lit by a single muted lamp. No furniture, but the walls were full of shadows.

There was something not right here, Raffy thought. Something he didn't like.

But his grandmother was already off, walking away from him with quick, decisive steps. Raffy squared his shoulders and followed her. When he saw what had frightened him, he almost laughed, but his laughter was immediately replaced by confusion.

Paintings, so big they reached from the floor to the ceiling. That was all the shadows were. Paintings so dark and bewildering Raffy almost couldn't bear to look at them, but which somehow he also couldn't *not* look at, like they were very loud and trying to tell him something. Paintings which were all lines – vertical, diagonal, side to side and top to bottom of the canvas, some whole, most broken, with rough surfaces, the paint applied in thick, uneven layers, with other things – pieces of wood, pinecones, a shard of glass, a crisp packet – embedded among the layers, piercing them with a terrible violence. As Raffy walked slowly past them, they gave him the feeling of a nightmare he used to have, of being in a forest at night, trees squeezing tight around him until there was no place left to run. As soon as he thought of the nightmare he understood what the paintings were, that the lines on the canvases were the trunks and branches of a smashed and broken forest, and he wanted to weep.

The corridor gave into a dark and cluttered living room, where his grandmother waited in front of another drawn curtain.

'Well?' she asked. 'What did you think of your grandpa's paintings?'

'My *grandpa*?'

Raffy's eyes darted around the room, as if a

hitherto unknown grandfather might jump out from behind the sofa.

Grandma's eyes narrowed as Martha stepped into the room behind Raffy.

'Martha, you have *told* Rafael about his grandfather?'

'I ... *Mum* ...' Martha's voice quivered. Raffy's eyes widened as he followed her gaze to a small table next to where Grandma was standing.

On the table was a group of photographs in silver frames. Eleven photographs, to be precise, one for each year of Raffy's life, and every picture was of him.

'Oh, Mum,' Martha repeated more softly.

'Lunch,' growled Grandma. 'Now.'

Over lunch in a tiny, paved garden, surrounded by pots of exuberant geraniums completely at odds with the strange tension of the meal in which Grandma talked a lot and Raffy and Martha very little, Grandma told Raffy about his late grandfather. He had been a great artist, she said, who had exhibited his works in galleries all over the world. A lover of nature and in particular of forests.

'Like Raffy,' murmured Martha, and Grandma nodded, as if she expected nothing less. The paintings were worth a lot of money, Grandma said, but she would not sell them, because it would be like selling a part of her husband, did Raffy understand?

No, Raffy did not understand, though he nodded and pretended that he did. Raffy didn't understand anything about this situation – why he was here, why he had never known about these grandparents. Why his mum and Grandma were talking about his dead grandfather rather than explaining eleven years of silence.

All Raffy could think, as he forced down his food, was that he did not want to be here.

After lunch, Grandma announced that she always had a nap after lunch. Raffy and Martha went for a walk.

By unspoken agreement, they kept silent until they had made their way through back streets and a little park to a canal, where they sat on a broken bench and watched a pair of coots paddle around a supermarket trolley upturned in the dirty water.

'We used to come here when I was little,' said Martha at last. 'If you go far enough down the towpath you get to the zoo. It was my favourite walk.'

Raffy didn't reply. Though in truth he was quite interested in the zoo, he was in no mood to talk about walks.

Martha sighed. How clumsily she had handled this, she told herself. But after all this time, was there any way of it *not* being messy?

'I'm sorry I didn't explain before we came,' she said. 'I thought it would be fairer for both of you this way.'

Raffy, bound by a lifetime habit of politeness and consideration, did not say what he wanted to say, which was that it would have been fairer for her to tell him he had a grandmother a long time before now.

Like when he asked her all those years ago if he had any family.

'Is that where you grew up, in that flat?' he said instead.

'No!' Martha sighed again, regretfully. 'We sold our old house after Dad died.'

'Your dad who did those paintings?'

Martha smiled. 'Horrible, aren't they? I wish Mum would sell them. She could move out of there if she sold just one of the big ones, buy a place with a proper garden – she loves gardens. But no, Joe Drori's widow doesn't do that. *Nothing* in the life of Joe Drori's widow matters more than his paintings.'

She delivered the last line with a bitterness Raffy had never heard in her before, and he didn't like it. One of the coots dived. Raffy felt a sudden, gut-wrenching longing for the cool clean waters of the pond at home.

'Shall I tell you what happened?' asked Martha.

Raffy nodded and dragged his mind back from Ravenwood. Martha pulled her legs up on to the bench and wrapped her arms around her knees.

'When you were a tiny baby,' Martha said, 'we lived at home with your grandparents and it was nice. They adored you, they had money, a big house – I wish you could remember it, Raffy, it was lovely. Full of light and books and plants, with plenty of room for all of us. But then Dad died, and it turned out we weren't as well off as we thought. Dad had debts all over the place, the bank was going to take back the house … Mum was grieving so hard, she could only just get through the days, but we had to do something. I mean, we needed somewhere to *live*. So one morning, after a night when none of us had slept, I called Dad's agent and instructed him to sell some of the paintings. But he told me he couldn't do it without Mum's approval, because they belonged to her now. So he called her and told her about our conversation, and …'

She paused. The coot bobbed up again.

'I've never known my mother so furious,' said Martha. 'We had a fight, we both said things we shouldn't, I was hurt and angry and so I left. Just to get my thoughts straight, you know? I was so confused – sad about Dad, angry about Mum, worried about where we were going to live. We used to go to the Yorkshire coast when I was little. It seemed a good place to go and think. So we went to the station and we got the first train there. I only meant us to stay a couple of days, but then we met Leo and … well, we stayed longer.'

'And you haven't seen her since?'

'Of course I have! I went back to fetch my things, I told her about Ravenwood. I helped her move house, I brought you a few times to see her, but … oh, it's a strange thing about grief, Raffy. You'd think that when two people lose someone they both love it would bring them closer together, but it doesn't always work like that, in fact sometimes it does the opposite. Grandma's so proud, you know, and for me – well, I think it was just easier to start again somewhere new. And we were both busy, she got a job in a doctor's surgery, I was teaching, I had you and Bea to look after … Our meetings grew further and further apart until they just … seemed to stop. I did send her those photographs, though. Every year, for your birthday. I sent her the photographs, and she kept them.'

Martha sounded sad now – sadder, thought Raffy, than he had ever heard her before, so that he felt sorry for her as well as angry. He reached out for her hand and she squeezed it gratefully.

'I'm really sorry, love. I know I should have told you all this before. It's just … the longer I didn't tell you, the harder it got. It wasn't fair.'

'No, it wasn't,' Raffy agreed, because it really wasn't.

It did explain things about his mum, though. Her passion for Ravenwood and her love for their family but also other things – like the way she wandered away alone sometimes from birthdays or Christmas to sit on her favourite bench, and was always so quiet when she came back. He had always thought Martha just didn't like parties but maybe, he realised now, she just missed her mum.

'How do you feel now?' asked Martha.

'I don't know,' he said honestly.

The bobbing coot was paddling back towards the shopping trolley, a plastic bag clamped in its beak. Raffy watched, feeling faintly sick.

London really was horrible.

'I think I would like to go home now,' he said. 'I think maybe everything might make more sense at Ravenwood.'

But he knew as soon as he said it that they wouldn't be leaving the city yet. Martha was looking down the towpath, and he could tell she was not seeing a dirty canal and a bird's nest full of plastic, but a path long ago with a little girl walking with her parents to the zoo.

'I booked our train for tomorrow,' Martha said. 'And I think Grandma would be hurt if we left so quickly. Now we're here, let's make the most of it, shall we?'

The weather had changed without them realising, the blue sky turned to grey, the thick London air close and heavy, difficult to breathe. Raffy, feeling a little mean, made a half-hearted attempt to change Martha's mind.

'I don't think it's fair to leave Noa alone,' he said.

'Leo will look after her,' said Martha. 'And it's only twenty-four hours. Why don't I show you a bit of London?'

What more could Raffy say? Martha clearly wouldn't change her mind. And so he followed her back through the dusty streets to a bakery she used to know where they stopped to buy pastries, and then to a park where people sweated under the heavy sky in which the emerald parakeets whirled, as out of place as Raffy.

Tomorrow he would be home, he told himself as they walked back to Grandma's flat through the stultifying dusk. He would go for a swim, and finish getting the treehouse ready for Bea, and soon she would come back and everything would be exactly like it was before.

Maybe.

Only twenty-four hours, Martha had said, as if twenty-four hours were nothing.

As if the whole world couldn't change in twenty-four hours.

CHAPTER TWELVE

Noa was invisible again.

Almost as soon as Leo returned from dropping Martha and Raffy at the station, he and Jack fought. They were on the terrace and Noa was in the kitchen, eating her breakfast in the armchair directly opposite the open door. They knew she was there. Jack and Ant had passed her on their way out. Ant had issued a jolly *good morning, young lady!* and Jack had nodded a terse *hello*. Leo had looked in too, when he got back. But none of them had thought it necessary to stop with her. Instead, they gathered outside, and now there was this fight, and they didn't even try to hide it from her. Noa couldn't hear what they said, but she could see them perfectly from where she sat. With her artist's eye for detail *she* noticed everything – Leo's clenched fists, the hair curling damply on his forehead, the sweat rings under Jack's folded arms. Ant neutral, sitting to one side, his legs crossed, a suede loafer balanced on the end of his foot, fanning himself with a folded newspaper.

After a few minutes, Leo raised his fist. With a bark of angry laughter, Jack ran down the steps and into the kitchen to grab his wallet and cigarettes and Ant's car key from the dresser, then stormed back out again to the terrace.

'You think you're leading such a wholesome life,' Noa heard him shout at Leo (except Jack used a lot of swear words), 'but the truth is you're the most selfish git I ever met. Why should you always be the one to get what you want?'

He marched across the meadow towards Ant's car, Ant himself following with a more measured step.

This time Jack had ignored Noa completely, and when Leo came back into the kitchen even he gave a start of surprise, like he had forgotten she existed.

Noa's throat tightened. It was just like the last long, lonely year at school.

'Noa,' Leo said, running his hands through his hair, looking thoroughly distracted. 'I'm sorry if you heard all that.'

'I didn't,' said Noa.

'Good, good ...' Leo cast his eye around the room, as if the kitchen might instruct him how to care for a solitary eleven-year-old guest.

'Look, will you be all right on your own for a bit?' he asked. 'Jack and Ant have gone out for the day, and I have to make some phone calls.'

'Sure,' said Noa. Then, with a touch of sourness. 'I am very used to being alone.'

'What will you do?'

'Sketch,' said Noa, even more sourly, and made a mental note of how she would draw Leo as he looked right now – like a hare caught in headlights, panicking but to box.

'Good, good ...' repeated Leo. 'Well, don't go down to the cove alone. I think the weather's changing. I don't want you down there caught in a storm.'

All morning, Noa obeyed. She went up to the tree house, where she sketched with a vengeance – not only Leo as a hare but also Jack, as a mean-looking hyena, and Ant complacent as a panther. When she grew hungry, she returned to the kitchen, cut some bread and cheese and took them out to the garden, where she sat on the steps to eat.

Leo was right, the weather *was* changing. The sky was leaden, the air heavy, the garden absolutely still. Even the birds were quiet. When something landed on Noa's bare thigh, she gave a yelp of panic and leaped up to shake it off. She huffed when she saw what it was – just a flying ant, the sort that herald a storm, as long as her thumbnail but harmless. She sat back down, then immediately jumped up again. The step was covered with ants, swarming around the crumbs from her lunch. She looked further across the terrace and her skin crawled. The ants were everywhere.

Noa didn't care now what Leo had said: she needed a swim. She fetched her towel and costume and fled to the cove.

The sea had changed too, under that leaden sky,

to a sullen, muddy green, strangely warmer than its previous sparkling blue. The tide was out, the high waterline marked by a debris of seaweed and plastic Noa hadn't seen here before. Thinking of Elva and Bea's Instagram dolphin, she walked the entire length of the cove, picking up the worst of the litter, which she dumped in a hollow at the foot of the path to bag up and take away later. Then, clammy with sweat, she went for a swim and spent the afternoon lying in the sea.

At about six o'clock, she climbed back up the cliff and stood by Skidbládnir. A swell was starting out beyond the cove, white crests running along the waves. With her hand on the dragon's neck, Noa turned back towards the garden. The flat grey sky had drained it of colour. For the first time, she noticed the ravages of the heatwave – the grass dry as straw, leaves curling on the trees. Not a breath of air . . .

She felt like she was the only person left alive in the world.

Back in the house, Noa went upstairs to shower, then returned to the kitchen where she helped herself to more bread and cheese, squashy strawberries and slightly stale chocolate biscuits. As she was putting her plate away, Leo appeared, even more dishevelled than when she had last seen him.

'Oh good, you've eaten,' he said. 'I'm so sorry. I've been on the phone all afternoon.'

He looked vaguely around the kitchen, again as if hoping it might offer clues of what to do with her. Wishing Martha were here to advise him.

'How about a game of cards?' he suggested, with little enthusiasm.

But the last thing Noa wanted was to play cards with someone who clearly considered it a chore.

'I think I'll just go outside,' she said.

She went back to Skidbládnir. Though it was still early, the sky was now almost completely dark, the crescent moon hidden behind the clouds rolling in from the sea. Still no air, even on the clifftop, but on the horizon lightning crackled, touching the sky purple. Very briefly, Noa wondered if she should go back into the house, but she dismissed the idea almost immediately. She had no desire to see Leo, or Jack and Ant when they returned.

She would stay here at Skidbládnir instead. Maybe she would even stay the night!

And so Noa climbed into the longboat and, after a tussle with the stiff bolt, opened the locker at the base of the mast. And as she took out cushions and a blanket to make herself comfortable, her eyes fell on the coloured glass lantern and the box of matches.

She hesitated a fraction of a second. *Don't play with fire* – wasn't that what grown-ups always said?

Then she lit a match.

The light cast by the lantern was as pretty as she had hoped, diamonds of green and red and gold which gave a carnival atmosphere to the dull night. Noa climbed on to a bench and held the lantern aloft, casting the shadow of Skidbládnir's curved dragon head across the grass. She hung it from a hook in the mast and stood before it. Her own shadow joined the dragon's. Dimly, she registered the sound of a car, doors opening and closing. She paid no attention to it, but began to sway.

On the multicoloured grass, the shadow girl danced around the shadow dragon.

And then the real magic . . . A soft beating of air in the still, still night, a ghost sailing towards her, a span of wings as wide as her own open arms . . . The owl no one had seen all summer floated to perch at the top of the mast and gazed down at Noa, yellow eyes bright in its round moon face. For a few seconds, they stared at each other. Then, with a single wingbeat, the owl took flight again across the meadow.

Noa watched it go, her mouth open with wonder. Then, forgetting her plan to spend the night in the longboat, she packed up and went back to the house.

A man was walking in the garden, along the edge of the woods. She paid no attention to him, but hurried on towards the house. She had to sketch this moment, which Skidbládnir had offered her like a precious gift. This moment when the owl had watched her and for the first time in over a year, Noa felt like she had truly been seen.

Later, when the police came, that was all she could remember.

CHAPTER THIRTEEN

B ea was having a simply marvellous time.

There had been a slight wobble, right at the beginning, when she was first reunited with her parents. Walking through the airport in Venice with Josh and Habiba, she had panicked. Had she made a mistake? She had come to make everything right, but would this trip be as disastrous as the last one? The panic worsened when she saw them. Josh's mother screeched as soon as he came through the gate and showered him with extravagant kisses. In contrast, Ingrid's quick peck, delivered from behind enormous sunglasses, felt disturbingly cold, the dry brush of Alex's cheek against hers positively icy. Bea tried not to think of Leo's hug when he left her at the airport, or Martha's when they said goodbye at Ravenwood. And oh! Ravenwood, she thought as she followed her parents across the terminal. Birdsong and the rushing wind and the cool greenness of Yggdrasil, the cries of the swallows, the goldfinches, the cove . . .

As Bea followed her parents to the exit, her heart bled for her lost summer.

But then . . .

Then she stepped outside the airport, and instead of a road and a car waiting to take them to the city there was a water taxi which sped Bea and her parents across a green lagoon, and very soon out of that lagoon there emerged a city of ice-cream coloured palaces, where church bells rang and shadows lurked, where sunlight glinted and where everywhere – *everywhere* – there was water.

'Do you like it?' whispered Ingrid.

Bea said, 'It's the most beautiful thing I have ever seen,' and Ingrid burst into tears. Bea tensed. How had that been the wrong thing to say? But then Ingrid threw her arms around her and hugged her just as tightly as Josh's mum had hugged him and said, 'Oh, darling, I'm so *glad*! You'll see, we are going to have the best of times!'

Bea's nerves had given way to tentative hope.

They did have a wonderful time.

A pizza eaten by a quiet canal, a dress bought in a tiny boutique. A church glittering with gold, a giant basilica in a vast piazza, a ride in a gondola. The scent of sweet jasmine, sunset over the Adriatic Sea, arriving at night in a medieval Croatian port, the smell of frying fish. The heat. A tiny hotel room overlooking a harbour, the taste of honey for breakfast. The warm sea, her cosy cabin . . .

Ice cream.

Bea loved everything, and she made a point of telling her parents so. The days passed and she must be doing something right, because the atmosphere on board the *Carolina* just got better and better.

Ingrid's laughter as the little yacht cut through the water, Alex's quiet approval at Bea's progress as a sailor. Huddling together over a menu in the evenings, *Bea, darling, you have to try the clams . . . the octopus . . . these sweet little cakes, this cheese, these figs . . .* Bea, who since Alex left her at

Ravenwood had hardly spent a night away from home, found that she relished not knowing where they were going to anchor from one day to the next. Her parents had a way of making everything beautiful. True, Bea held back a little. She was loud in her appreciation of what they gave her, but quickly learned that any mention of Ravenwood, Martha, Leo or Raffy brought a shadow to Ingrid's smile, a slight tension to Alex's shoulders. Easier, she found, not to talk about them at all, and to send her messages home in secret. Holding back and being secret did not come naturally to Bea, but she managed it because it was important. For five whole days, she lived in the delightful bubble of her parents' love, and nothing else mattered.

Bubbles, however, have a tendency to burst.

On the last day of their trip, the *Carolina* re-entered Italian waters. Early in the evening – as Raffy and Martha walked back to Grandma's through London streets and Noa went out to Skidbládnir beneath a storm-bruised sky – the *Carolina*'s crew sailed her into a tiny harbour south of Trieste for their final night on board. Then, after showering and changing into their best clothes, they went out for dinner.

Later, Bea would think that Ingrid had behaved strangely all evening. That her laugh was louder than usual, her enthusiasm a little forced. She would piece events together and remember that her mother's hands were never still. She would tell herself that she had known something enormous was coming, but the truth was that at the time, as she skipped off the *Carolina* into the crowded village in her new green dress, Bea thought only of what she was going to eat.

They sat in a little square where the trees were hung with fairy lights, at a table covered with a white paper cloth.

'A celebration!' Ingrid cried, fanning herself with the menu. 'Because we are such brilliant sailors!'

The waiter brought drinks, wine for Alex and Ingrid, lemonade for Bea. They clinked glasses.

'To us,' said Alex, with an awkward smile.

'To us!' cried Ingrid, beaming, and, 'To us,' Bea echoed, not quite sure what she meant but pleased that it made her parents happy.

It was a good evening. They talked about sailing, about tomorrow's itinerary and the villa where they would be staying next week. The food, when it came, was delicious. As they ate, they grew sleepy and found they had less and less to say, but it didn't matter. On a low wall across the square, a teenage boy was playing the guitar, and they listened to him. Ingrid swayed to the music. Bea wondered about asking for guitar lessons.

It was lovely.

Alex's phone rang as they were finishing dessert.

'It's Jack,' he said, looking at the screen.

Ingrid put down the spoon that was raised halfway to her mouth.

Bea would remember that, later.

It was noisy in the square. Alex turned away to take the call, shielding the phone with his body in order to hear better, then got up and walked towards the trees.

Bea suddenly felt like she had eaten too much.

'Something's happened,' she said.

'I'm sure it's nothing,' said Ingrid.

Alex returned to the table. A look passed between

him and Ingrid, and a tiny nod. Later, Bea would definitely remember that, but she didn't register it then because she was right.

Something had happened.

Something terrible.

CHAPTER FOURTEEN

After weeks of hot dry weather, it took minutes for Skidbládnir to go up in flames.

It was Ant who raised the alarm. Noa, sketching the owl on her window seat, heard him shout as he ran across the meadow.

'Fire!' Ant yelled. 'Out at the longboat! Fire! Fire!'

Noa froze, pencil in hand. She heard footsteps, Jack and Leo running from different parts of the house.

Fire, at Skidbládnir?

In a daze, she knelt to look out of the window.

'I'll get the hose!' Jack cried, as he ran across the terrace.

'It won't reach!' Leo shouted from inside the kitchen. 'I'll get the fire extinguisher.'

Out towards the cliffs, Noa saw a faint glow. Skidbládnir? But how?

Jack and Leo were running back. As if from a great distance, she heard Leo shout that the fire extinguisher had barely touched the flames, then registered that Ant was taking command.

'Jack, call the fire station,' he ordered. 'Tell them the flames are already out of control. Tell them that the sand around the base of the ship is containing the fire for now, but it won't for long. And let's get out there with more water. Leo, find containers, we'll form a chain to fill them. Get Noa to help, I know she's just a kid, but it's all hands on deck for this. How the hell did this actually start?'

The lantern, thought Noa. *Oh God, the lantern!* Had she blown it out, after seeing the owl? She *thought* she had ...

Dimly, she heard Jack on the phone to the fire service, Leo running through the house. He burst into her room, gabbling at her to fetch pans, buckets, anything she could grab from the kitchen, while he fetched more from the barns.

'Run!' he shouted, as she stared at him. 'Noa, run!'

They did exactly as Ant ordered. Fetched every container they could find which Noa filled from the hose and which Leo ran to Jack, who ran them to Ant, who threw them over Skidbládnir, and maybe it did slow its progress but – three men and a girl, fighting a fire in a heatwave which had baked the country dry for weeks? It wasn't enough. The blaze spread and spread and spread some more, until the flames reached the prow and the dragon head was belching flames.

'How far is the fire station?' asked Noa.

'Town,' panted Leo.

Town, where Noa lived. Where there was school, and home, and Dad and Tamsin and the twins and the new flat.

Town which was over an hour away, and the flames were starting to lick their way up the mast . . .

A shadow ran across the lawn towards her, followed by another, and another. Ghosts, thought Noa, wildly. Ghosts, fleeing Skidbládnir . . . but why was Leo smiling like that, like he might cry?

'Neighbours,' said Leo. 'Oh, God, neighbours! Who called them?'

'I did,' said Jack. 'At least, I called the pub.'

Harry the publican and Magda from the Nature Society and Elena the librarian; Nick, parents from school, the volunteers from the village shop. They poured across the lawn to join the chain, bringing their own pails and buckets, and now nobody was running but passing water up and down the line, and it was amazing, but it still wasn't enough. Skidbládnir was a furnace, its wooden structure black and crackling, flames blazing orange against the purple sky.

With a belch of sparks, the mast exploded.

Moving as one, the crowd ran back. Then, from a distance, ready to run further if need be but too appalled to leave, they watched.

When the rumbling started, Noa thought the ship itself was groaning. Almost inaudible at first against the shouts of the crowd, it gathered strength until the very ground appeared to tremble.

Closer and closer, the flaming wood spun through the night towards the parched dry grass. Louder and louder, the rumble grew until, with a blaze of lightning which lit up the burning longship and a crash of thunder which seemed to call it home, the sky tore open and it began to rain.

Oh, how it rained! Water poured out of the sky and put out the flames, it soaked into the desiccated earth, it flattened flowers and bowed trees, it filled the thirsty ponds and streams. All over the countryside, people came out of their houses and held their faces up to it. At Ravenwood, the pails and buckets were abandoned. The villagers threw their arms in the air and danced in a circle in the sodden meadow.

'No way of knowing for sure how it started,' said a firefighter back in the kitchen, after the crew had checked the blaze was well and truly out. 'Anyone here smoke?'

'I do,' said Jack. 'But I wasn't anywhere near the boat. I'd been out for the evening, we'd just come home.'

Noa swallowed. 'There was a candle,' she whispered. 'Could that have done it?'

'A candle?' The firefighter frowned. 'What, just on its own? Seems unlikely.'

'It was in a lantern.' Noa swallowed again, trying to remember. 'I mean, I think I blew it out ... I'm almost certain I put it all away, but ...'

But there was this owl ...

The firefighter patted her hand. 'Like I said, no way of knowing for sure.' She turned to Leo. 'The police will come tomorrow, they'll have a few questions. Just a formality, but they have to do it. You do want to be careful with things like lanterns though, especially in this hot weather.'

But I was careful, thought Noa. *Wasn't I?*

'I know.' Leo's face was ashen now, his elation following the rain replaced by deep exhaustion. 'It won't happen again.'

'It's not your fault, Noa,' Ant said when the firefighters had gone. 'Accidents happen, even to grown-ups. You mustn't blame yourself.'

'Of course she mustn't blame herself,' snapped Leo. 'I'm the one who left her alone all day when I should have been looking after her. I'm sorry, Noa. I shouldn't ... I mean, I should have ... I mean, if it's anyone's fault, it's mine. God, what a day. I need a drink.'

Noa watched in disbelief as he sank on to a chair and with shaking hands poured himself a glass of brandy. Was that really all he had to say? Were they all going to accept so easily that the fire had started because of her?

Ant and Jack poured themselves drinks, then left the kitchen. Noa hung on a little longer, hoping that Leo might talk to her when they were gone, but as soon as the the door closed behind them he reached for his phone to call Martha. Sick with shame and burning with a sense of injustice, Noa went to her room where, fully dressed, she curled into bed with her sketchbook.

For a while, she ran her fingers over her half-completed drawing of the owl, trying to piece together exactly what had happened. But the events of the evening were too hazy, blurred by exhaustion and emotion. She abandoned the owl and began to flip back through the pages. Past drawings of poor Skidbládnir which brought a lump to her throat, of the tree house which also made her want to cry, of Bea as a witch and Raffy as a mouse which felt like a lifetime ago – back, back, back, until she found what she was looking for, a picture copied from a photograph when her mum had first given her the sketchbook, of herself as a smiling little girl with her hair in pigtails, holding hands with her parents. Noa blinked. She had no idea, that little girl, how badly one day everything would go wrong.

Quietly, her face buried in her pillow so no one would hear her, Noa began to cry.

CHAPTER FIFTEEN

Back at the *Carolina* after dinner, on the seating area on deck, Bea wept as she hadn't wept since being brought home early from the French holiday.

Ingrid tried to comfort her.

'But everything is all right, darling,' she said. 'Nobody was hurt. And Leo can build another boat.'

Ingrid glanced at Alex and blushed slightly as she said this, but Bea was too distraught to notice. How could she make her parents understand what Skidbládnir meant to her? That even if Leo built an exact replica, it would not be made from *her* oak, the one which in falling had brought her to Ravenwood?

Even now, she was afraid of upsetting them! With a great effort, she stopped herself crying.

'I still don't understand how it happened,' she said.

Alex repeated what he had already told her. Noa had been playing with the lantern in Skidbládnir. She had forgotten to blow it out, somehow it had fallen and with everything so dry because of the heatwave, the fire had caught fast. It was a miracle the rain came when it did.

Bea listened, but it didn't make *sense*. She thought of Noa's tidy bedroom, the neatness of her clothes and hair.

'Noa's just not like that,' she said. 'She always puts everything away. It's like she can't help herself.'

'Well, it seems that this time she didn't,' said Alex. 'Evidently she admitted as much to the fire services.'

'Nobody is saying she did it on purpose, darling,' said Ingrid. 'Personally, I think Leo was very irresponsible, leaving her alone all day.'

But this made no sense either.

'Noa was alone all day? Where was Raffy?'

'Raffy is in London with Martha,' said Alex. 'They have gone to visit Martha's mother.'

Bea began to feel as she had when she went ashore at the end of her first day on the *Carolina*, like everything around her was swaying, including the ground beneath her feet. How could she not know that something so momentous had happened to her best friend?

'Raffy has a grandmother?'

She thought about her argument with Raffy the night before she left, and the fact that in all the days since she had had no direct contact with him. How was he feeling now? She needed to talk to him, badly. Cry with him about Skidbládnir, about this sudden grandmother ... She should call him, on Martha's phone. But there was nowhere private to go on the little *Carolina*, and the thought of her parents hearing her conversation was just wrong. She slumped back into her seat in despair.

'I think,' said Alex, 'we should stop talking about all this and go to bed.'

Bea lay in her bunk for ages, unable to sleep. Two messages had come through. Leo had written to say I imagine your parents have told you about the fire – I'm so sorry. Not sure how it happened but it's wretched. Martha had written that she hoped Bea wasn't too sad, with no mention of her mysterious mother. Neither message felt satisfactory.

Oh, it was so hot! For the first time since coming away, her little cabin felt not cosy but stifling. Bea thought longingly of the storm at Ravenwood. The smell of the woods after the rain! Martha – Martha, who kept such enormous secrets! – had once said that she would bottle it if she could. Bea and Raffy had macerated leaves and bark in a bucket for weeks, trying to turn them into perfume, but the result had been a foul-smelling sludge. The memory made Bea smile.

She fell asleep and dreamed of forests.

Just before dawn, her phone woke her with a *ping*. It was a message from Noa. A short message, just two words, but infinitely more troubling than Leo and Martha's commiserations.

I'm sorry.

Bea stared at the screen.

How should she reply? By saying it didn't matter? But it did matter. It mattered a lot. The thought of Skidbládnir burning made Bea feel physically sick.

Should she tell Noa it wasn't her fault? But it was her fault, wasn't it? If Noa was saying she was sorry, didn't that mean she had done it?

Except that it still didn't make sense.

I don't understand what happened, she wrote.

There was quite a long pause before Noa replied.

I saw the owl.

It was on the mast and it looked at me. I sort of forgot everything else.

That might do it, thought Bea. *The owl nobody had seen all summer, watching you from the top of Skidbládnir. That might make you lose your head, though it doesn't explain how the fire actually started.*

How are things at Ravenwood? she asked.

Awful, Noa replied. Leo and Jack are fighting, and Martha and Raffy can't come back from London because all the rain caused a landslide and now the trains aren't running.

A pause. I wish you were here.

And then None of this would have happened if everyone hadn't gone away.

Another pause. Bea? Are you there?

But Bea still didn't know what to say. Skidbládnir

and the owl, the fire ... She tried to picture them all in her mind, and they felt like a film of somewhere very far away.

What was it like, the owl? she asked at last.

Like a ghost, Noa replied. Like a spirit, like a messenger from another world. It was beautiful.

A messenger ...

A seagull cried outside the *Carolina*, the first one of the day, its cry exactly the same as the gulls of Ravenwood. Bea's heart tightened. It was not so hard to think that it was relaying a message sent across half a continent.

What message, though?

That something here was wrong ...

Another ping. Noa was waiting for an answer.

I want to see the owl too, Bea wrote. I want to come home.

All day, as the *Carolina* sailed briskly back towards Venice on the final leg of her trip, Bea's longing for Ravenwood grew, an all-consuming homesickness. *You can come home whenever you want to*, Leo had told her at the airport. Her parents would understand if she asked them – wouldn't they? Alex had cut the French trip short when Ingrid was upset. He could do the same for her. She just needed to find the right words, to be sure not to hurt their feelings.

There was a moment, as they approached Venice and saw the floating city once more emerge out of the waves, when she almost changed her mind.

'You know, they call Venice the *Serenissima*,' Ingrid whispered. 'It means, *the very peaceful one*. It's wrong, of course. Its history is as brutal as most of Europe's. But when you see it like this, you can understand, can't you?'

Yes, in that moment all Bea wanted was to fold herself into Ingrid's arms and hold on to her forever. But later, when the *Carolina* was returned to the boat hire company and she found herself alone in a hotel room overlooking a busy square, the longing for home overwhelmed her again.

She would tell her parents how she was feeling, she decided as she came out of the shower. She would explain, and they would understand.

She put on her new green dress, knowing it would please Ingrid, then went out on to the landing and knocked on her parents' door.

'Is that you, Bea?' cried Ingrid.

Bea gave herself a shake and went into the room.

And her whole world turned upside down.

CHAPTER SIXTEEN

'Darling!' Ingrid, in a crisp white dress, was sitting at a dressing table applying mascara. 'How pretty you look! Isn't it absolute heaven to be properly clean again? That little shower on the *Carolina* just didn't quite cut it, did it?'

Bea sat down on the edge of the bed with her hands beneath her thighs.

'I need to tell you something.' She looked around. 'And Dad.'

Ingrid put down her mascara, picked up a tube of lipstick, then put that down too.

'Of course. He's just getting dressed. Alex, darling! Bea's here.'

She picked up the lipstick again and applied the

colour to her lips. Alex, freshly showered and in clean clothes, came out of the bathroom.

Bea's parents' eyes met in the mirror. A tiny nod, and just before Ingrid spoke again, Bea remembered that other nod in the restaurant last night, after Alex had spoken to Leo, and how all evening her hands had never stopped moving . . .

Suddenly, despite the heat of the day, she felt cold.

'Actually, Bea, darling . . .' Ingrid stopped to collect herself. Alex crossed the room to stand beside her. Ingrid took a deep breath.

Bea wrapped her arms around herself with a sense of creeping dread.

'Actually, Bea, darling, there's something we need to ask *you*,' Ingrid said. 'Do you mind if we go first?'

She rushed on without waiting for an answer.

'I expect you have been wondering, darling, why we asked you on holiday.'

'I . . .' Bea didn't know what to say. She *had* wondered, of course, especially at the beginning. And if she hadn't felt this new need for home, she might be pleased to know. Now though, the question felt like a distraction. 'Maybe a bit . . .'

Ingrid ploughed on.

'We have been thinking about . . . No, we have *decided* . . . What I mean is, it's not really a question any more, it's . . . Bea, darling, you're going to come and live with us!'

Shock does strange things to a person.

Bea's head swam, her vision grew blurry and her ears rang. She pressed her hands into the bed, her fingers curling into the embroidered flowers of the coverlet as if this could stop the sense of falling.

Breathe, she told herself, the way Martha had taught her once after she fell down the steps on the terrace. *Breathe.*

This was good, wasn't it? Astonishing, also, and unexpected, but good – no? It meant her parents wanted her. They loved her! Bea had made things right.

Why, then, did it feel so wrong?

'You're about to start secondary school,' Ingrid was gabbling. 'There's a really good one near us.'

A new *school*? thought Bea, bewildered. 'But I'm going to Meadowbanks next year with Raffy.'

Ingrid looked pleadingly at Alex.

'This is a much better school than Meadowbanks,' he said, as if this somehow made sense. 'They have really excellent facilities, and terrific results. We spoke to the head teacher before coming away and she says they have a space for you.'

Wrong, thought Bea, *wrong, wrong, wrong.*

'You spoke to the head teacher before coming away?' she stammered. 'But why didn't you tell me?'

Too late, Alex realised his mistake.

'It seemed ... sensible,' he said. 'You know. We wanted to ... make sure.'

'Make sure of what?' Bea's head began to swim again.

'You know ...' Alex swallowed. 'That we all got on.'

Got on ... thought Bea, the words echoing round her head. *Got on, got on, got on* ...

'We just think it's time ...' Ingrid's voice quivered. 'You know, darling ... we've been apart so long. We think it's time you came home. We want ... we want to look after you.'

Home, thought Bea, and suddenly she knew what was wrong. Of course she did. It was obvious.

'The thing is,' she said, carefully, because it was important for her parents to understand, 'I can't live with you, because I already have a home. That's what I wanted to talk to you about. I've had a lovely time but I'd like to go back now, please.'

Another look between her parents, and Bea's sense of dread solidified.

'There's something else,' she said. 'There's something you're not telling me.'

She watched her parents' fingers intertwine as Ingrid's hand found Alex's.

And then they told her.

Jack's friend Ant wanted to buy Ravenwood, and Jack, Leo and Alex had just agreed to sell it to him.

CHAPTER SEVENTEEN

Martha broke the news to Raffy in Grandma's flat. She sat him down on the sofa beside her and held his hands, and though her eyes were red from crying she tried for his sake to be calm.

At first Raffy only felt numb. Martha spoke, and he tried to grasp what she was saying, but it was impossible to understand, or to believe that life could so suddenly change. Discovering Grandma, the incomprehensible news that Noa had burned down Skidbládnir, the awful frustration of not being able to rush home because of the landslide. He had done his best: tried not to weep too much over Skidbládnir, accepted the train situation. Made friends with Grandma, though it had been difficult at first.

They had gone to a market together this morning, walking uncomfortably side by side, and neither of them had any idea what to say to each other. But then she had bought plums, ripe greengages which they had eaten in the garden, licking golden juice off their fingers. He had told her about the plum trees at Ravenwood, and how in late summer he and Bea shook the fruit out on to sheets held by the residents of the retirement home who came to help in the garden. Grandma had listened with interest and responded by telling him about her own grandmother's mango trees. Then, after her lunchtime nap, she had taught him to play backgammon. She had beaten him roundly in every game, and each win had put her in a better mood. By the end of the fifth game she had been so pleased with herself she had opened a tin of chocolate biscuits. It had been annoying but also quite funny, and he had enjoyed himself. In his head, he had begun to introduce Grandma to Bea – he was quite sure they would get on – and to show her round Ravenwood.

But now this! No, it was impossible to understand how a day could change so fast.

'I'm afraid it's all a rush,' Martha said. 'Ant has big plans for Ravenwood. He wants . . . he's going to turn it into a hotel. He wants to start work by the beginning of the autumn.'

Autumn, thought Raffy. *Autumn, autumn, autumn.*

Autumn at Ravenwood meant a back-to-school picnic at the cove for their friends, and blackberry picking in the hedgerows. It meant the swallows leaving and nights drawing in, a Halloween party telling ghost stories in the woods. Mowing the meadow and trees losing their leaves, scarlet berries blazing in the leafless hedgerows.

So all of this would be gone, would it?

Huh, thought Raffy, with absolutely no emotion.

'Love?' Martha was looking at him, her face full of concern. Raffy realised she was expecting a reaction.

'Why?' he asked.

Strange, he thought, licking his lips, how dry his mouth felt.

'You mean why are they selling?'

Raffy nodded. Martha drew her legs up and hugged her knees.

'Jack's wanted to for a while.' She paused to steady herself. She had to be strong. It was what she *did*. 'He needs money. He actually asked Leo last year to buy his share of Ravenwood, but Leo told him he couldn't afford it. Jack asked Alex too, but Alex also said no, because it was Bea's home. It was all a bit awkward, I don't know if you remember? Jack let it rest for a bit, but then he came back.'

Grandma, who had been listening from the kitchen with a mixture of indignation and disapproval, came in carrying a tray of tea and handed them each a mug.

'I gave you both three sugars,' she huffed. 'Drink. It will do you good.'

She sat on an armchair opposite them, glaring at Raffy until he had taken several sips. He licked his lips again, a little uncertainly. The tea had helped with the dryness, but brought a fresh problem: as his body relaxed, feelings began to trickle back.

Specifically, rage.

With great effort, he tried to focus on his mum.

'The night before Jack came to us at Ravenwood,' Martha was saying, 'he had dinner with Ingrid and Alex. That's when they told him they were thinking of bringing Bea back to live with them. And then Jack spoke to Ant – you know, that day when they were all supposed to come . . .'

'When Noa arrived?' Raffy forced himself to whisper, to stop himself from howling.

'Exactly, when Noa arrived.' Martha hadn't touched her tea. Now she paused to drink it all in one go, then stared into the bottom of the mug, gathering her thoughts. A broken Leo had explained everything to her in painstaking detail on the phone, but it was hard to find the words.

'Just say what happened,' advised Grandma. 'That's what your father always said to do. If you're stuck, just say it straight.'

Martha nodded, and went on.

Instead of getting the train as planned, she told them, Alex, Ingrid and Jack had spent that afternoon with Ant, who said that if they wanted to sell Ravenwood, he might want to buy it. Ingrid and Alex had asked for time to think. They wanted Bea to live with them, but they weren't absolutely sure it was the right thing to do.

'It's not,' growled Raffy.

Martha, though she agreed, didn't allow herself to be deflected.

Off Ingrid and Alex had gone to Venice to think, she continued wearily, and Jack had come to Ravenwood to give Leo a last chance to buy his share, but Leo still couldn't afford it. They had had a fight over breakfast that first morning – did Raffy remember how suddenly Jack had left?

Raffy nodded, swallowing a painful lump at the memory of that perfect day with Bea and Noa at Ravenwood. How blind they had been to what was going on!

After the fight, Martha said, Jack returned to London with a tablet full of photographs for Ant, who came back with him to have a good look around before making his offer to buy. By which time, Ingrid and Alex asked Bea on holiday to see if they all liked each other enough to live together.

Raffy exploded. 'You mean like a *test*?'

Grandma snorted. She had tried to contain her reactions until now, but this was too much.

'Did anyone actually ask the child what she wanted?'

Martha, who had put exactly the same questions to Leo when he told her, almost broke as she tried to be fair.

'I think they meant to, but then the fire happened ...'

'The fire?' Raffy was utterly bewildered. 'What does that have to do with it?'

'It made Ingrid decide Ravenwood wasn't safe,' said Martha. 'And once they decided that, Alex agreed to sell Ravenwood. And then it was two brothers against one and Leo didn't really have a choice. He can't afford to buy Jack's share, let alone Alex's as well, and we can't afford to keep Ravenwood going without Alex's help.'

She held back what she had told Leo – that he should stand up to his brothers, that they couldn't force him to sell. Leo, shaken by the fire and convinced that he was to blame for not supervising Noa better, had not wanted to listen. Now she took Raffy's hand, though whether to reassure him or herself was hard to tell.

'We'll find somewhere nice to live,' she said, trying to sound positive. 'I promise. Once the sale goes through, we will find somewhere lovely …' She trailed off. Raffy wasn't listening, and even to her own ears, the words rang false.

'Does Bea *have* to live with them if she doesn't want to?' Raffy demanded.

'I suppose they can't force her if she doesn't want to,' said Martha doubtfully.

But what if Bea *did* want to? thought Raffy. Or worse – what if Bea, to please her parents, agreed to live with them even if she didn't want to?

He wriggled out of Martha's arms.

'You have to stop it,' he said. 'All of it. Selling Ravenwood, Bea going. Mum, you have to *do* something. It's our home! They've no *right* …'

But here Martha finally broke. It had become painfully clear to her in her conversation with Leo that there was nothing she could do. After Jack's first visit, she had offered Leo her savings and together they had looked at raising a mortgage, but her earnings were too low and Leo's too erratic to get the sum they needed for Jack's share of Ravenwood. And though she had begged Leo not to sell, two things had become clear: the first, that without Alex's support they could not afford to carry on running Ravenwood. And the second, that it was not Martha's decision to take, because however much she loved Ravenwood and called it home, it did not belong to her.

Raffy stared, aghast, as she began to sob. He had never seen his mum cry before, other than watching films, which didn't count. That sort of crying made him and Bea laugh. This was different. This . . . he had no idea what to do.

With a grunt, Grandma pushed a tissue into Martha's hand and instructed her to blow her nose.

'But why?' she asked, when Martha had regained control of herself. 'Why does this man Jack want to sell Ravenwood?'

Martha sniffed. 'He wants to build a house in Costa Rica.'

'But he already has a house in Costa Rica!' cried Raffy. 'With monkeys and hummingbirds and that sloth in the tree!'

'That house isn't actually his,' said Martha wanly. 'He's been living there while the friend it belongs to was abroad, but now she's coming back and Jack wants a house of his own.'

'Jack is selling our house so he can build one for himself?'

The rage now was too much. Raffy jumped to his feet and kicked his grandmother's sofa, not once but several times. Grandma winced, but didn't intervene. She could see it was what he needed to do, to stop his heart from breaking.

CHAPTER EIGHTEEN

After the first shock of her parents' announcement, Bea had locked herself in her hotel room. Now she sat on the floor with her back against the door, while Ingrid on the other side implored her to come out.

'Darling, it's Venice!' she begged. 'We're only here one night, and there's still so much I want to show you!'

Bea balled her fists and pressed them into her eyes.

'I don't care.' She had given up trying to be nice to her parents. 'I'm not coming out.'

How could Ingrid still think Venice mattered, when she and Alex had just blown her whole world apart?

'*Please*, darling!'

'Let me handle this.' Alex stepped up to the door. 'Bea, this is your father! I am ordering you to come out of your room. Let's talk about this like civilised grown-ups.'

'For your information,' said Bea, with unpleasant sarcasm, 'I am not a grown-up.'

Alex, unused to such extreme parenting, shrugged helplessly at Ingrid. Ingrid, stroking the door for want of being able to stroke Bea, said, 'Darling, we are going to wait right here until you come out.'

'Then you'll wait a long time,' snarled Bea. 'Because I'm only coming out to go home.'

Ingrid's face crumpled. Alex took her gently by the arm.

'Come on,' he said. 'Let's go for a walk.'

'We can't leave her!'

'It will do us all good to cool down.'

They left, Ingrid promising they would be back soon. Bea listened to their footsteps walking away, then banged her head against the door with a howl of mirthless laughter. Everyone knew you didn't leave children alone in hotels. And they said they wanted to look after her!

She pushed herself up and went to the bed to fetch her phone from her bag. She had to speak to Leo, now, at once. Maybe – she was clutching at straws here – maybe he would tell her none of this was true.

Straight to voicemail. With a cry of frustration, she shoved her phone into her pocket and went to stand by the open window.

Ravenwood, sold! How could Leo agree to this, how could he? As for her parents asking her to live with them ... oh, it was too confusing! To have wanted so much to know they cared about her, and now for them to show it like this! By ripping her away from her home! By *selling* her home! Without even asking what *she* wanted! And all that stuff about *we just wanted to make sure we got on* that Alex had said. Bea thought of Leo's hug at the airport, of Martha holding her after the French trip, of Raffy who always looked out for her even when she was horrible. *They* never needed to make sure. They just loved her.

All this time, since the French trip, thinking she had done something wrong, and they *just wanted to make sure*!

Her phone pinged. A message from Noa.

I just heard. I'm so sorry.

Bea huffed as the last thread of hope deserted her.

Another ping from Noa with a sad face emoji, and then the words Your parents are definitely more rubbish than mine.

With a bark of laughter, Bea tapped out No way am I ever living with them. Or staying on this stupid holiday. I'm coming straight home!

Another message, straight back.

How?

It was a fair question. Bea had no idea how she would do it, but she *had* to go home now, there was no question about it. She had to speak to Leo in person, make him change his mind. If she could only show him how much she cared, he would do it for her, she was sure of it. Leo could never resist her anything.

But how, how, how? How *did* you go home, when you were a child, underage and with no money?

Her room looked over a little square, lined with bars and cafés. Brow furrowed in thought,

Bea watched the outside tables begin to fill with customers ... oh!

Waiting in line in front of an ice-cream shop, a shock of yellow hair. Was it ...? Bea leaned out a little further – yes, it was!

'Josh!' she shouted.

Several people looked up. She pointed towards Josh, who was shuffling forward, his eyes glued to the display of ice creams.

'Josh! Up here! Oh, please, somebody get him!'

A man in the queue tapped Josh on the shoulder, and at last he looked up, shading his eyes with his hands. He beamed when he spotted her, then waved at her to come down, gesturing that he would buy her an ice cream.

'I got you chocolate,' he said, handing her a giant cone as she ran out towards him. 'I was at the front of the queue and couldn't wait, so I just thought, *everyone likes chocolate.*'

'I couldn't actually eat a thing.'

'Really? Then I'll have yours. There's a canal through that archway. Let's go there. It's cooler by the water.'

As they walked over to the canal, Josh explained that – as predicted – his parents had got bored with the villa within a few days and decided to come to Venice instead.

'And *I'm* bored of looking at churches, which is all they want to do when they come here. So Mum gave me her credit card for ice cream and told me not to get lost. She's very good like that.'

They emerged from a stone passage by a small, quiet canal where they sat on the ground with their feet dangling over the water.

'What are *you* doing here?' Josh asked, finishing his own ice cream and embarking on Bea's. 'Have you already been sailing?'

'Oh, Josh!'

He listened in very un-Josh-like silence as Bea told him everything.

'But what about the bats?' he asked when she had finished.

'I don't know, but Ant doesn't sound like the sort of man who would like sharing with bats.'

'I suppose most people wouldn't,' Josh mused.

'Josh, help me! I have to go home! I have to change

Leo's mind, but I don't know how.'

'How to change Leo's mind or how to go home?'

'Both,' admitted Bea. 'But first, getting home.'

'Well, I *am* an expert traveller.' The second ice cream finished, Josh licked chocolate off his fingers as he began to think. 'You can't fly ... you saw how much they check on us. A runaway kid's got no chance of flying alone incognito. And the bus is too slow. As soon as they realise you've gone they'll have police looking all over Europe for you, and you'll probably still be in Italy when they catch you. No, you need to be fast. You need to be invisible. You need to ... I've got it!'

He stopped pacing.

'*What?*' asked Bea.

'You need to catch the night train to Paris!' Josh grinned and held up his mum's credit card. 'I'll pay.'

CHAPTER NINETEEN

It took Josh less than a minute to research what time the train left (in less than an hour) and Bea less than five to pack what she needed into her rucksack (her blue hoodie, toothbrush, passport, phone and charger, a book, her water bottle, the few euros she had). Ten minutes to run, weaving through crowds, over bridges and canals to the station, three to find the ticket office . . .

'You'll have to change stations in Paris to catch the Eurostar train to London,' Josh panted, as they got into the queue. 'But hopefully we can buy you a ticket all the way from here.'

'Won't you get in trouble with your mum?' asked Bea.

'To be honest, she probably won't even notice,' said Josh. 'They're very rich, my parents. Mum might even be pleased. She loves trees and things.'

'If you're sure . . .'

'Well, I'm not *sure*,' admitted Josh. 'But listen – the thing is to look really confident, like we are absolutely allowed to do this.'

The person before them finished their transaction and left. Chins up, credit card at the ready, Josh and Bea strode forward.

'I'm sorry,' said the ticket seller, not looking sorry at all. 'I cannot sell international tickets to minors.'

'Oh, but my mum's just coming,' said Josh. 'She's just at the, um, shops.'

The ticket seller narrowed her eyes.

Glumly, they walked away from the desk and stood on the concourse, surveying the platforms.

'So that's that,' said Josh. 'Look, there's your train, just sitting there, all ready to take you back to rescue Ravenwood. Honestly, when I'm a grown-up, I'm going to ban rules. Grown-ups are allowed to do stupid things all the time yet here *we* are, trying to save the world, and nobody's letting us. It doesn't make sense. Bea, where are you going?'

'I just want to see,' said Bea.

There were no gates to go through to the trains. You could just do as Bea was doing now, stroll right on to the busy platform where two guards were checking passengers' tickets before they boarded.

She glanced at the clock. Five minutes till the train left.

Her mind started to race.

'Josh, will you do something for me, if I ask you?'

Josh didn't bat an eyelid. 'Whatever you want,' he said.

Bea positioned herself directly opposite one of the train's doors, then looked up and down the platform. Most of the passengers had already boarded, but there were still a few stragglers left. One door down towards the front of the train, a guard was helping a large family climb up, the mother holding a baby, a boy about Bea's age holding a toddler by the hand, the father hauling a pushchair and assorted pieces of luggage. One door down towards the back, half turned away from her, the other guard was arguing with a large, bearded man with a big rucksack on his back and a patch over his right eye, apparently about the man's bicycle.

But the door opposite Bea was empty.

'OK, don't be too obvious,' she said. 'Just tell me when you're sure the guards aren't watching.'

Josh's eyes widened. Bea tried to look brave. How scary was this plan, really, compared to jumping off a cliff?

'I ... Bea, you're not ...'

'Just do it, Josh.'

With a resigned shrug, Josh stuck his hands in his shorts pockets, lowered his eyes and watched the guards. Heart thundering but absolutely concentrated, Bea continued to stare at the door.

A whistle blew. A voice announced the train's imminent departure.

Come on, thought Bea. *Come on, come on, come on ...*

She had to do this. She had no choice. How else was she going to get home?

'*Now!*' hissed Josh.

Bea dashed across the platform and leaped on to the train. Seconds later, the doors closed behind her.

Sometimes all you can do is jump.

For about ten seconds, Bea stood exactly where she was, her whole body ringing with the shock of what she had just done. Then, as the train began to accelerate, she forced herself to think.

She was on a train, in a foreign country, with no ticket and almost no money. She needed to hide – but where?

As discreetly as she could, Bea took stock of her surroundings. She was in a corridor. On one side, windows. On the other, doors to six-person compartments consisting of two benches facing each other. Everywhere, passengers coming in and out, organising themselves.

What should she do?

She stared out of the window, feigning interest in the last sights of Venice as the train raced over the lagoon, her mind racing again. In the toilets? She had read about people doing that in books. It might work for a bit, but all the way to Paris? It was an awfully long time to stay in a toilet. Surely someone would notice?

A woman with a small child came out of a compartment and looked at her curiously. Bea cursed inwardly. She knew that look. She had seen it on Martha about a million times – any minute now, the woman was going to ask if she was all right. She turned away sharply and walked with as much purpose as she could in the other direction, past the bathroom and into the next carriage. But now here was a guard, hurrying towards her! Eyes on his phone as he advanced, but very soon he would look up ... Bea squared her shoulders, trying to appear confident as she peeped into the compartments, searching for one that was empty ... There! Before the guard saw her, as if by miracle!

Bea dived in and closed the door behind her, then threw herself into the corner seat, let out a long breath and closed her eyes ...

But not for long.

With a click and a creak, the door swung open again. The compartment darkened. The large man with the beard and the eye patch was standing in the doorway.

At first, neither of them spoke. The man nodded. Bea nodded back, then took her book out of her bag and pretended to read, watching out of the corner of her eye as he settled in.

It took a while. The man shrugged off his rucksack then put it down on the bench opposite Bea's, untied the top section and took out a canvas bag. He stowed the rucksack in the overhead rack, then sat down in the window seat. Out of the canvas bag, he took a chequered napkin, which he spread over the little table by the window. On to the napkin he put a tin plate, and on to the plate he carefully unwrapped waxed paper containing cheese and salami. Next he took out a loaf of bread, which he put next to the plate, then a thermos flask, a bar of chocolate, a bag of tomatoes and a punnet of plums.

Bea's tummy rumbled.

The man cleared his throat. Bea dragged her eyes away from the page and tried not to flinch. The man's one good eye was fixed on her. He spoke, in heavily accented Italian. Bea shook her head. He spoke again, in English.

'I said, I wonder if you are in the right compartment.'

Bea gave a tiny nod and prayed that he would believe her. Also, that he wouldn't ask where her parents were.

The man pulled an apologetic face.

'What I meant was, I *know* you are in the *wrong* compartment, because I booked this one for my own exclusive use.'

He's going to call the guard, thought Bea in a panic. *Or my parents. Or the police. He knows that I have run away ...*

The man was still talking, apparently unaware of her distress.

'I take up rather a lot of space, you see, and it's more comfortable for everyone if I travel alone. Name's Fortescue, by the way. Major Fortescue, currently on a train and cycling holiday, though for the sake of accuracy I must acknowledge it comprises rather more train travel than bicycling. And you are?'

Bea's mind was in overdrive now, trying to make sense of the situation. Who was this person? Why was he being nice? Should she tell him her real name? No, she decided. She should not.

Her eyes swept the compartment for inspiration and landed on the picnic table.

'Plum,' she said hoarsely. 'Bella . . . Plum.'

'Plum,' he repeated.

Bea tried to hold the major's gaze, then jumped as her phone shattered the quiet of the compartment. She slid it out of her bag and looked at the screen.

Ingrid.

She put the phone back in her bag. When it had finally stopped ringing, the major cleared his throat again.

'The thing is,' he said, 'I saw you give the guards the slip in Venice.'

Bea gasped. With a delighted grin, the major leaned forward, his elbows on his knees.

'Come on, Plum!' he said. 'What's the game?'

Bea's tummy rumbled again. The major's grin grew wider as he gestured to the seat opposite his, on the other side of the table.

'Please,' he said. 'Share my picnic. We've about an

hour till Padua, when the guard comes to check our tickets. You can talk while we eat.'

Through villages and vineyards, the train sped on. The light outside began to fade. In the darkening compartment, Bea talked and the major listened.

Far behind them in Venice, Alex and Ingrid began to walk back to the hotel.

CHAPTER TWENTY

'So, on the one hand,' said the major, waving his flask, 'we have a house, a garden, a pond and a lot of birds. On the other –' waving his cup – 'a lawbreaker, an accomplice, a potential international police operation and people who care for you who must be beside themselves with worry.'

'I know!' Bea felt a pang of guilt, then steeled herself. It wasn't her fault Leo and her parents had made these terrible decisions. 'But you have to understand how special Ravenwood is. It's not *just* a house and a garden, and it certainly isn't a hotel, it's . . .' She stopped, her throat tight.

'It's what?' asked the major.

'Home.'

'Ah.'

The major put down the cup and flask and sat back with his hands over his knee, thinking.

'The world is full of people doing what you are,' he said at last. 'Crossing borders in the shadows. Many have lost everything and home is something they carry only in their hearts. You have family who love you, you are safe. One way or another, you *will* have a roof over your head.'

Bea flushed. 'You think I'm spoilt.'

'Not spoilt,' he corrected. 'Just more fortunate than many.'

Bea thought about this.

'Of course you're right,' she said after a while. 'I know I'm lucky. And yes, it is unkind to make people worry about me. But Major Fortescue, Ravenwood is *precious*. And we have to fight for the precious places, don't we? It might not change the world for everyone, but it's a start, isn't it?'

The major nodded, and his smile was kindness itself. 'It *is* a start, Plum. It is a very good start indeed.'

Again, Bea's phone shattered the air.

'My mother,' said Bea, looking at her screen.

Ingrid was probably back at the hotel by now, had probably realised Bea wasn't in her room. She was probably beside herself.

Bea's finger hovered over the answer button, but she didn't press it. The phone stopped ringing, then immediately started again.

Alex.

'In a few minutes,' the major observed, when again the phone stopped, 'we will arrive in Padua. All you have to do is cross the platform and you can be back in Venice in an hour.'

'What do you think I should do?'

'The choice,' the major said gravely, 'is entirely yours.'

Already, the train was beginning to slow. Bea put her phone down on the table.

'My uncle can track it,' she said. 'Does that still work if I switch it off?'

'With the right technology,' the major said, 'I believe anything is possible.'

No one else got off at Padua. Clutching her phone, Bea ran across the platform and jumped on to

another train, looked around for the right place ...
Just inside, near the door, there was a luggage rack.
For a few seconds, she dithered ...

But she didn't have long.

At floor level beneath the luggage rack, there was
an enormous suitcase. Bea pushed the phone behind
it, then scrambled back out and across the platform.
She burst into the major's compartment just as the
departure whistle went.

'That was close,' said the major mildly, as she
collapsed panting on the seat opposite him.

Bea grinned. 'You know, you're really not like
most grown-ups.'

'I should think not,' he grumbled, but she could
see that he was pleased.

The guard came. Bea, lying flat under the major's
bench, clutching her rucksack and only breathing
when she absolutely had to, listened as the two
men conversed.

'There will be a passport control at the Swiss
border,' said the guard after he had checked the
major's ticket. 'I am sorry, but we will have to
wake you.'

'Of course.'

'The restaurant car will be open shortly, should you wish to dine with us.'

'Thank you, but I will go to bed soon.'

'The pasta is good. Also the wine.'

'Nonetheless, I need my beauty sleep. I am not getting younger. Or indeed any more beautiful, ha ha.'

'Ha ha,' responded the guard, and then he was gone.

After a few minutes, the major said, 'You can come out now, Plum.'

She crawled out, spitting dust.

'Goodness, you *are* dirty,' he observed. 'You'd better go and clean up once our friend has finished his rounds. We'll talk about your battle plan shortly. First ...'

'My battle plan?'

'You can't just go haring off without a battle plan, Plum,' the major said severely. 'You say you want to talk to your uncle, but what happens if he doesn't want to listen? Sadly, talking isn't always enough. If your first plan fails, you'll need allies, reinforcements. We can discuss this later. More immediately, we need to talk about how to get you home. I'm afraid I have to leave the train before Paris. Is there anyone in the city who can help you?'

'Help me what?'

'Get to England,' the major said patiently. 'Come on, Plum. *Think*.'

Bea thought. Paris! The major might as well have asked if she knew anyone on the moon. Except . . .

Who had talked to her about Paris recently? Something to do with art. No, with school. With art school! Noa's marvellous sister Elva! Once arrested for spraying a polar bear on to a government building.

'There is someone,' she said. 'Maybe. Can I use your phone?'

'What shall I tell her?' she asked, when she had tapped what she hoped was Noa's number into the major's phone.

'The truth?' he suggested.

Bea wrinkled her nose. 'The truth feels very complicated.'

'Then make it simple,' said the major.

Bea thought a bit, then began to type.

On my way home! she wrote. I'll be in Paris in the morning. Do you think your sister would help me?

Noa replied immediately.

Of course. What do you want her to do?

'Take you across Paris and put you on the Eurostar train to London,' said the major, when Bea asked him. 'There'll be some sort of paperwork to sort out too, what with you being a minor. Tell her to look into that.'

Bea tapped out a message to Noa.

Promise not to tell ANYONE.

I PROMISE, Noa replied.

Bea gave his phone back to the major. She wished there was a way she could tell Raffy what she was doing, but there wasn't. And he would understand. As soon as he heard she had run away, he would know that she meant to save Ravenwood. And when the time came, he would help her.

From a police station in Venice, with an ashen Ingrid by his side, Alex called Leo. When Leo had finished shouting at him for losing his daughter – *how had it happened? how?* – he remembered that he could track Bea's phone.

'She's heading south,' he told Alex. 'She's somewhere near Bologna.'

Then he called Martha.

Martha was washing up after supper as she answered the phone. When she heard that Bea was missing, she dropped the glass but made no move to pick up the shattered pieces. Instead, she stumbled from the kitchen to the living room, where after flapping about in a very un-Martha way, she began to make calls. To Alex, to Ingrid. To Bea, who of course didn't answer. She went online in case the landslide situation had changed (it hadn't). She called Leo again. She began to cry.

Raffy tried to hide his feelings as he helped Grandma finish tidying the kitchen, but as soon as everything was put away he stepped out into the garden and hugged himself.

All day, since Martha broke the news about Bea and Ravenwood, he had felt desperate. But now!

Bea had been right, that Raffy would know what

she was doing. He had known from the moment Martha told him she had gone missing.

She was coming home, and she was going to stop Leo selling Ravenwood. Everything was going to be all right.

'I am puzzled by your reaction.'

Raffy jumped, then watched in uneasy silence as Grandma stomped towards him.

'You cried and cried when your mother told you about the sale and the girl going to live with her parents, and you've been miserable all day. But now everyone's in uproar because she's gone missing and you seem positively *pleased*.'

Raffy jumped again as Grandma's hand shot out and grabbed his.

'Something's up,' she hissed. 'Your mother's too agitated to see it, but I'm not blind. Come on, out with it! Where is she?'

'I don't know!' With some tugging, Raffy managed to free himself.

Grandma narrowed her eyes.

'I don't!' he insisted. 'I just . . .'

With a loud huff, Grandma sat down in one of the

metal chairs by her little garden table, and yanked Raffy into another.

'Has this girl been in touch with you?' she demanded. 'Because if she has, I want you to tell your mother. This instant, Rafael. She and I have had our differences, but I won't have her worried like this.'

'I swear, Bea hasn't been in touch!' said Raffy. 'It's just that . . .'

How could he explain in a way that someone who didn't know Bea would understand?

'Oh, out with it, child!'

'Bea makes things happen,' said Raffy.

Grandma raised her eyebrows. Raffy tried to think of an example.

'Like, when she was a baby, even before she could talk, she made her dad leave her at Ravenwood.'

Grandma's eyebrows went higher. 'I sincerely doubt that's true.'

Raffy thought harder.

'All right, so once we were playing in the woods at home and I fell out of a tree. I broke my nose, and there was blood everywhere and I nearly fainted. Bea tried to carry me, but I was too heavy. So she went to get the big wheelbarrow from the barn and she pushed me back to the house. It was really hard, because we were only little, but she did it. Then when we got back she said I'd tripped over a football. Do you see what I mean? That's Bea. If there's a problem, she fixes it.'

Grandma was looking nonplussed.

'Why didn't she just fetch your mother? Or her uncle?'

'We weren't supposed to be playing in the woods,' Raffy explained. 'Mum had this thing about one of us drowning in the pond. We weren't actually meant to be climbing trees either.'

Grandma pursed her lips. 'So she's a liar.'

'I suppose so,' Raffy admitted. 'But only when she needs to be. Mostly she's completely honest. And brave. Like when we jump off the cliff she goes way higher than me. And also, going sailing with her parents, that was brave too. I didn't think so at first, but now I do. It may not seem brave, going on holiday with your parents, but if you knew how much they've upset her, you'd understand.'

Grandma sniffed.

'I suppose she does sound unusual.'

'Maybe,' said Raffy. 'I don't know. She's my best friend. Like my sister. And I swear I don't know where she is or what she's planning but I do know she's going to stop them selling Ravenwood. She's going to save it for us. I don't know how, but she is.'

'Hmm,' said Grandma. 'And it's that special then, this place? Special enough to cause all this trouble?'

She sounded unconvinced, but when Raffy wriggled round to look at her properly he saw that she was really listening, with her head to one side just like Martha did.

'Grandma, it's the most special place in the world!' he breathed. 'If you could see it, you'd understand. It's like paradise. It's like . . .' He looked at the cracked paving stones of the patio where daisies had seeded, blown in on the wind. Thought about the trapped London trees towering over the pavements, the coots building their nest on the dirty canal, the parakeets multiplying in the parks. Nature everywhere was unstoppable, but nowhere more than at home.

'It's the most alive place you ever saw,' he said.

There was a pause while Grandma considered this.

'I used to have a sister,' she said. 'She was older than me, and fierce. There was a boy at school who used to pick on me – pulled my hair, tripped me up, that sort of thing. My sister found me crying one day after he stole my lunch. She was so incensed she punched him. The school punished her, but she didn't care because he never troubled me again.'

Raffy tried to imagine his Grandma as a small girl crying. It was impossible.

'What happened to her?' he asked.

'She died a few years before you were born.'

'I'm sorry.'

Grandma shrugged sadly, like she was saying this is what happens in life, people die.

'Grandma? Could you not mention to Mum, about the wheelbarrow and falling out of the tree? You're the only person I've ever told about it.'

Just for a second, his grandmother's eyes grew bright with tears. It was over so fast, Raffy thought he must have imagined it. But this time, when her hand took his, it was gentle.

*

After the train left Milan, Bea and the major went to sleep, stretched out on the benches and wrapped in the blankets provided by the train company. A few hours later, the train stopped and they woke. The major lifted the window blind, then nodded at Bea.

They were at the Swiss border.

Without a word, she threw him her blanket, took her rucksack and slipped once more beneath the bench.

Shortly afterwards, there was a knock at the door. The major unlocked it and, muttering a sleepy greeting, handed over his passport. A few words were exchanged in a language Bea didn't understand, then the door closed and the major locked it again.

'Welcome to Switzerland, Plum,' he whispered.

'Switzerland!'

Bea knelt on the end of her bench and peeped out behind the blind. Outside, she saw a deserted platform, another train, a dim light. Beyond that, solid darkness.

'Mountains,' said the major. 'Some of the tallest in Europe.'

'I wish I could see them.'

'You will, Plum. One day you'll come back in daylight, and you'll see that they are beautiful.'

CHAPTER TWENTY-ONE

The compartment was bright with light when Bea woke the following morning, the countryside outside gently hilly, dotted with low stone farmhouses. The major's rucksack was strapped and buckled on the seat by the door. The major himself sat by the window, drinking from his thermos cup, a plate of pastries on the table before him.

'Good morning, Plum, and welcome to France! I bought us breakfast from the restaurant car. Now listen up. I've had a scan of the British, French and Italian news, and there's nothing about you anywhere, but it doesn't mean no one's looking for you. We will shortly be arriving at my stop. I need to leave you now to fetch my bicycle. You know what to do next?'

'Keep a low profile,' Bea yawned, as she sat up. 'Be discreet.'

They had planned for this.

'Exactly.' The major grunted and held out an envelope. 'I've written down Elva and my telephone numbers, and the address of the British consulate in Paris. The consulate's very much a last resort. I've given you all the money I have on me too. It's not much, but it will get you a taxi there if you need it. Any questions?'

Bea shook her head. There were many questions she would have liked to ask, but there was also a lump in her throat which made it impossible for her to speak.

Fifteen minutes later, the train pulled into a station. The major raised his hand in a farewell salute.

'Never forget the precious things, Plum.'

'I won't,' whispered Bea.

From the window of the corridor, Bea watched the major wheel his bicycle along the platform. He was possibly the strangest person she had ever met. She hoped very much that she would see him again.

Feeling suddenly very exposed, she returned to the compartment and opened her book. The words swam before her on the page but, knowing how much grown-ups approve of children reading, she did not look up again until the train approached the suburbs of Paris.

The plan had sounded so straightforward when Bea and the major had discussed it.

'Avoid drawing attention to yourself,' he had told her. 'Get off the train with a group of other passengers and make sure you're never alone. That big family who got on just before us in Venice – try to look like you're a part of their group, though not so close that they'll get suspicious. Keep looking ahead – you're not some gawping tourist, you're a kid going home with her family. You *know* Paris. Elva will be waiting at the end of the platform. When you see her, no big surprise or excitement. Just say hello and walk away together, like you're old friends. Above all, try to look confident.'

It was *hard* for Bea not to gawp though, as she climbed down from the train. Her first time in Paris! She wanted to drink it all in – the high ceiling made of glass and wooden slats, the

French advertising hoardings, the holidaymakers in brightly coloured clothes rushing about the platforms. But she had to concentrate. The family from Venice were climbing out now. She waited for them to pass her, then slipped in behind them, looking straight ahead . . .

No!

Two police officers, gun holsters all too evident against their tight-fitting uniforms, stood by the top carriage. She would have to pass them to get off the platform . . .

Should she run? Get back on the train? Hide? Impossible, they would notice! No, she must just keep walking – chin up, *confident*, as if every inch of her skin was not prickling, as if breathing did not hurt, as if her legs were not about to collapse beneath her, and *hope* . . .

The police officers turned away before she passed. Dizzy with relief, Bea walked on.

Only a few more steps now and she would find Elva, Elva who was so marvellous, who would take her across Paris to the London train, Elva . . .

Who was not there.

Bea gripped the straps of her rucksack. What had the major said?

Elva will meet you at the end of the platform.

Elva had confirmed it just a few hours ago in a message to which she had attached a photograph of herself, a young woman with light brown skin like her sister's, dressed in blue dungarees and yellow hi-tops, hair in a messy ponytail, nose pierced with a pink diamanté stud . . . Bea had studied it thoroughly.

The end of the platform – could that mean at the back of the train? That made no sense. Even so, Bea cast a discreet glance behind her, peering through the last stragglers from the train.

No Elva.

Blood was pounding in Bea's ears now, but she tried to stay calm. She needed somewhere to hide and think.

The Venice family were heading noisily towards the station's exit. Bea followed them as far as a gallery of shops then, after checking quickly that no one was watching, dived into an alcove behind a vending machine.

Something growled.

Bea shot out again. From a safe distance, she peered behind the machine. Two pairs of eyes – one human, one dog – stared back at her from a pile of blankets on the ground.

'Sorry,' Bea stammered. Then, remembering something from the smattering of French she had learned at school, '*Pardon.*'

She shuffled away and went to stand before a chocolate shop, where she pretended to look at the window display. From her pocket, she took the envelope the major had given her, containing money and telephone numbers. Maybe she should try and call Elva. But how? She looked around for a payphone. Did such things even exist here? And would she know how to use one if they did?

Wham!

Bea stumbled as a woman – white, middle-aged, definitely *not* Elva – clipped her shoulder rushing past.

'*Oh, pardon, ma puce!*'

The woman held Bea by the arms to steady her, checking that she was all right, then with an apologetic smile hurried off again. Bea watched her go – looked again at the clock, fumbled again for the envelope in her pocket.

Her heart missed a beat. It wasn't there.

Bea turned until her back was against the glass of the shop window, bracing her legs to stop herself sliding to the floor. The woman . . . the woman had stolen the envelope. And now Bea had nothing.

She wouldn't cry, she told herself. Crying wouldn't help. She just needed to keep on being discreet and come up with a plan. What, though? She scowled as she tried to think.

'Bea?'

Bea jumped as she heard her name. Then, with a howl of relief the exact opposite of low profile, she threw herself into the arms of the young woman in front of her.

Elva had finally arrived.

CHAPTER TWENTY-TWO

Elva was cheerful, breathless and full of apologies for being late. She had wanted to take the Metro but found her line was closed, she had caught a bus but the traffic was jammed, in the end she had got off before her stop and run. Imagine how she felt when she had arrived and found no sign of Bea!

'I had to hide,' Bea said. 'In case the police saw me and asked questions. A woman stole my money.'

'Oh, you poor little squirrel!' said Elva, so kindly Bea hardly minded at all being called a squirrel. 'What a horrible time you've had. Let me just tell Noa I've got you. Everyone's doing their nut about you, by the way. They found your phone in Naples! Noa says your uncle's in pieces. Should we call him now to let him know you're safe?'

Bea wrinkled her nose. She didn't like to think of Leo being in pieces because of her, but it *was* his own fault for agreeing to sell Ravenwood. And calling him might ruin everything.

'No,' she said. 'He'll only call my parents, and then they might make you keep me here until they come to fetch me.'

Elva nodded as she tapped out her message to Noa.

'Right, that's sent.' She pocketed her phone. 'Now listen. Our train's not till this afternoon ...'

'You're coming with me?' Bea's heart gave a leap of gladness.

'I'm afraid so,' said Elva. 'Under-twelves can't travel alone on Eurostar. It's the rules. I've thought and thought about it, and I can't come up with any other way of doing this. It *would* be good though if your uncle or someone could pay me back. You know, me being a penniless art student and all. You don't mind me coming with you?'

'No!' Bea grinned. She already adored Elva. 'I'm pleased. It's all been a bit scary, to be honest. And I'm sure my uncle will pay you back.'

'Onwards, then!' Elva beamed. 'We've got about four hours. How about I show you Paris?'

Bea would never forget her first visit to Paris. She and Elva walked for hours. There was the River Seine sparkling in the summer sun, there were stone bridges and cobbled streets, bright shops, café terraces crowded with people. There were sandwiches of crusty bread eaten by a fountain in a park, and ice cream eaten in front of a glass pyramid before a museum which had once been the home of a king. But there were also other things Elva quietly pointed out, which would remain etched in Bea's mind for a long time after she left the city.

The slogans painted on walls and pavements, the ugly comments sprayed on a shop window. The queue in front of a trestle table where two women were serving soup, the man in rags asleep on a bench.

The alcove beneath a flight of stone steps built into a hillside, a scrap of material pulled across it like a curtain, where they stopped and Elva called out in French. The curtain which parted to reveal a woman sitting on a mattress, making beaded bracelets with two little girls. The girls' smiles as Elva shrugged off her rucksack and brought out coloured paper and broken crayons for them, then a thermos flask and a packet of sandwiches for their mother. The hugs between the two women.

She would remember her conversation with Elva when they left the woman and her daughters and walked to the top of the hill, where they sat on a bench with the city spread out at their feet.

'Do they live there, on that mattress?' asked Bea. 'Isn't it dangerous?'

'For now,' Elva replied. 'And yes, it is dangerous.'

'Why do they stay, then?'

Elva sighed. 'Because there was a war in their country, and they lost everything? They're supposed to have a room in a hostel, but something went wrong and they're still waiting for it. Meanwhile – there *is* nowhere for them to go.'

Bea would remember the silence, while she thought about what it meant, to lose everything and have nowhere to go, and what she said next to Elva.

'All of this, that I'm doing for Ravenwood. Is it silly?'

'How, *silly?*'

Bea picked her words with care. 'Major Fortescue said, when I told him why I was running away, he said that I'm fortunate. That other people only have homes in their hearts.'

'And what else did he say?' asked Elva.

'That we have to fight for the precious places.'

'Well, then.'

A weak sun broke through the clouds. Elva sighed again.

'We do what we can, Bea. And when we've done that, we try to do a little bit more.'

'Maybe one day, the girls under the steps can come to Ravenwood,' said Bea.

She would remember Elva's smile.

'Maybe they can, Bea.'

*

Outside the Gare du Nord, where they were to catch the Eurostar, Elva stopped to give Bea her ticket and tell her what was going to happen next.

'We'll go through three sets of checks,' she said. 'First we scan our tickets through a machine, then there's the French and the British borders where they check your passports. Those are the tricky bits. As a minor, you're supposed to have a letter from your guardians authorising you to travel. I did think of forging one, but that would actually be a criminal offence and would probably get me arrested again, which I really don't want. So we're just going to have to hope they won't notice, but if they do, don't worry, OK? I'm sure we can talk them round. And then, whoosh! Only two hours to London.'

For the first time, it occurred to Bea just how much Elva was doing for her. And the major too – what would have happened to him if the guards had found out he was hiding her?

'Will you get into trouble?' she asked. 'Even without the forging? Like will they think you're *kidnapping* me?'

'Maybe.' Elva grinned, but Bea couldn't help

thinking she looked nervous. 'But it's worth a try, isn't it? So come on! Best foot forward, as my mum would say!'

But Bea had another question.

'Why are you doing this?' she asked. 'You don't even know me. You've never *been* to Ravenwood.'

Elva squeezed her hand. 'Much as I like you, Bea – and I really do – I'm not doing this for you. I'm not even doing it for Ravenwood, though I agree that precious places are important.'

'Why, then?'

'For Noa, of course,' said Elva, as though that were obvious. 'Now chin up, shoulders back! Try to look . . .'

'Confident,' Bea said with a smile. 'I know.'

One day, she would pay back all these new friends she was making.

Including Noa.

Bea and Elva did everything they could to appear innocent. In the queue to scan their tickets, they shared headphones. Waiting to go through French border control, they ate sweets. And when it was

Bea's turn to step forward, though her tummy was churning, she handed over her passport looking just the right amount of bored.

They needn't have worried. The border officer barely even glanced at their papers before waving them through.

Two steps completed. Only British border control to go.

Just look relaxed ... Bea went first, Elva waiting behind her. Handed over her passport, trying to breathe normally as the border officer scanned it ... The officer smiled, typed something into her computer, asked idly if Bea had been on holiday, had she enjoyed herself?

Yes, Bea replied, she had, very much.

Had she been anywhere nice?

Yes, said Bea without thinking, she had been in Italy, sailing.

The border officer said how nice, and who was she travelling with? Bea, with her heart in her mouth, said 'my friend' and pointed at Elva. The border officer smiled again. Then frowned.

'No luggage?' she asked.

They were asked to step aside, and another officer was called to ask more questions. What exactly was Elva's relationship to Bea? Did she have a letter authorising her to take Bea across the border?

Elva, who until now had been so cool, floundered. She was just taking Bea home, she said. She was doing the family a favour, no one had thought about a letter of authorisation.

It was perfectly obvious she was lying.

Bea tried to speak. Elva held up a trembling hand.

'Let me handle this, Bea.'

'But . . .'

'We'll come to you soon, sweetie,' said the border officer. Her tone was not unkind, but it was dismissive. As if, even though Bea was the one being kidnapped, what she said didn't matter.

But this was her fight, not Elva's. It wasn't right for the older girl to be getting into trouble. And surely, now, she had come far enough? Only two hours to London, Elva had said! Surely now they would not send her back to her parents now?

She cleared her throat. Nobody listened. She cleared it again. At last they turned towards her.

'Please,' said Bea. 'This is all my fault, not Elva's. Perhaps you could phone my uncle?'

PART THREE

CHAPTER TWENTY-THREE

When the border police called from Paris, Leo's knees actually buckled and he only just managed to fall into the chair in the hall where the house phone was kept.

'You *knew*!' he stammered afterwards to Noa, who was listening not so secretly from the top of the stairs. 'You must have. How else would Bea get in touch with your sister?'

Noa couldn't deny it, so she said nothing.

'And you didn't tell us!' said Leo. 'Even after all that Naples business!'

There was a pause as they recalled the scenes in the middle of the night, Bea's phone tracked to a railway siding hundreds of kilometres south of Venice, Bea herself nowhere to be seen and every adult member of her family in tears.

'And all the while she was on her way to Paris!' Leo ran his hands through his hair. 'What for, I would like to know? I mean what *possessed* her?'

He swore – softly but very rudely – then once again picked up the phone to Bea's parents.

Noa fled.

Alone in her room, she checked her own phone. There was a message from Elva, confirming what the border police had agreed with Leo – that an officer would accompany Bea to London, where she would be delivered to Martha.

Quite the adventure, Elva concluded cheerfully. Let me know what happens next. Keep up the good fight! Love you, pipsqueak.

Love you too, Noa tapped back. Thank you for helping.

So that was that, she thought. Bea had done it. She had got herself across Europe and she was coming home. Hopefully – Noa didn't know how – she would convince Leo to change his mind and not sell Ravenwood.

Suddenly she felt exhausted.

In the two nights since the fire, Noa had barely slept. Every time she closed her eyes, she saw the Skidbládnir burn again, the flames leaping into the night sky, the sparks spitting from the mast as it began to fall. When she did manage to sleep, she had nightmares in which it didn't miraculously rain but the fire spread like a devouring monster towards the house . . .

All because of her.

She was glad Bea was coming home and she really hoped her plan to talk Leo out of selling Ravenwood would work, but more than anything right now, Noa wanted to call her mother. Capable, clever Mum, who didn't always get everything right but never let Noa doubt she loved her. But the news from the hospital where she was working wasn't good. More and more people were arriving every day whose homes had disappeared in the earthquake, and the sickness was spreading. It was the reason Leo hadn't called her after the fire, and the reason Noa wouldn't call her now.

Dad, then . . .

She scrolled back through her old messages.

Just to let you know I'm here, if ever you need/ want me xxx

Should she call him? But what for? To ask him to fetch her away to Tamsin's house? No, she still couldn't bring herself to do that.

But how much longer could she stay at Ravenwood? She had adored it here from that very first morning swimming with the seal – maybe even her first afternoon, sketching in poor burnt Skidbládnir – but didn't the fire change everything? People kept saying it wasn't her fault, but how else would the fire have started?

Did anyone really want her here?

Noa curled into her favourite spot on the window seat and closed her eyes.

She was so very, very tired of not belonging.

The sky was still overcast after the rain, and the breeze coming through the open window was cool. Noa shivered, then sniffed, remembering how her dad always laughed at her when she was smaller for refusing to wear a jumper even when she was cold.

'Do star jumps, then,' he used to say, before

jumping with her himself in encouragement, pulling silly faces to make her smile.

Oh, she thought with a sudden sob, she missed him *so much*.

She *would* call him.

She pressed his number at once, before she could change her mind. She would tell him about the fire, and maybe if he was alone without Tamsin he would listen to her the way he always used to, very seriously, like what she said really mattered. And then, though she understood he wouldn't come and stay with her at the flat, maybe – *maybe* – he would come to Ravenwood and they could spend some time together. She could tell him how she was feeling. She could explain about the fire and the nightmares, how scared she had been and how worried that it was all her fault, and he would give her a big dad hug and it would feel like everything was all right, the way it used to.

Maybe.

The phone rang only twice before someone answered.

'Noa?'

Noa slumped. It was Tamsin.

'Is that you, sweetheart? Your dad's driving, he asked me to pick up. Sweetheart, are you OK? Can you hear me?'

Noa ended the call and threw her phone across the room on to the bed. The worst thing about Tamsin was that she was so *normal*. Noa would have understood – maybe – if her dad had left because he had fallen in love with someone even more incredible than her mother. But Tamsin was deeply, deeply ordinary. Apart from the small matter of stealing Dad, she was even – though Noa hated to admit it – nice.

Well, Noa wasn't ready yet to be nice back, however desperate she was feeling. With a frustrated huff, she picked up her sketchbook again and, a little guiltily, began to draw another witch – a grown-up one, with Tamsin's face . . .

At about five o'clock, Leo went out on to the terrace with a drink. Jack joined him shortly afterwards. Old habits dying hard, Noa listened to their conversation.

'We'll be off soon,' said Jack. 'Back in the morning before nine.'

Noa frowned, then remembered – Jack and Ant were going away for a night to a country hotel on the other side of town, something to do with research for Ant's plan to turn Ravenwood into a hotel. Abandoning the witch, she began to draw a clock face, the hands set at nine o'clock, sketching in Jack's thin nose and bushy eyebrows to make the clock look like him.

On the terrace, the brothers sat without talking while Jack lit a cigarillo and began to smoke. Noa turned the clock hands into smoking matches.

'Look,' said Jack, as he exhaled. 'I know this isn't what you wanted . . .'

'Not what I wanted!' said Leo, incredulous.

'. . . but it's for the best, you'll see. You'll find a nice place to live . . .'

'I've *got* a nice place to live!'

'. . . that's not falling apart. My bedroom ceiling . . .'

'It's on my list of things to do! I was just waiting for Nick to help me when he finished the tree house.'

'You can't keep patching up the place with the help of an old man, Leo. Ravenwood needs money. Think how great it's going to look – like old times! Ant will bring it back to its former glory.'

'I happen to think it's glorious now.'

'It's a mess, Leo! The lawns, the flower beds . . .'

'It's not a mess, it's a wilderness! Which your *mate* is going to destroy. I've seen him, pacing about the place with his plans. He'll undo everything Martha and I have achieved here. I know this isn't exactly Costa Rica but . . .' Leo paused to steady himself. 'All I'm saying now is you could have waited before . . .'

Two things happened quickly, one after the other.

Jack said a thing so terrible that for a few seconds Noa felt her heart stop. When it started again, she looked properly at her drawing.

Matches. *Smoking* matches. Fire.

Out of the corner of her eye, Noa caught a glint of gold. She turned to look at it and caught her breath.

A spider, like a tiny parachutist, floating on a thread.

She flicked back through her book until she came to the picture she had drawn on her very first night. What had she said to Raffy, when she showed it to him?

What sort of person calls hummingbirds 'little flying jewels' but kills a tiny, floating spider?

Yes, that was it.

What sort of a person did that?

A few minutes later, Noa slipped unnoticed through the front hall and out to the garden. Avoiding the terrace, she went round the back of the house and hurried through the meadow to the cliff where Skidbládnir had stood. Nothing remained of Leo's beautiful ship but a few charred pieces of the heavier timber. Noa crouched and touched the blackened grass, her throat tight but her blood pounding.

If she could only find what she was looking for . . .

If she could only be right . . .

Centimetre by centimetre, Noa searched the ground, raking through the ashes until her back ached and her hands and knees were filthy. But, as the sun dipped towards the sea, she was forced to admit defeat. She had covered the whole site of the fire, lifted each piece of burnt and twisted wood, searched every crack and cranny in the ground, but she had found nothing.

CHAPTER TWENTY-FOUR

Bea's train had arrived a few minutes ago and the first passengers were already coming through the arrivals gate at St Pancras International.

Raffy, standing beside Martha, was furious.

In his mind, since running away from Venice, Bea had grown to the stature of a Valkyrie, those Norse warrior goddesses who could have eaten uncles and their miserable friends before breakfast before restoring the world to its rightful order. And this was good. They needed a Valkyrie right now, because the news from Ravenwood was getting worse by the minute as the plans for Ant's hotel came to light. Countless trees in the woods were to be felled to make way for luxury cabins, the pond was to be turned into a swimming pool, large sections of the meadow concreted over for tennis courts, and now ... Raffy clenched his teeth. Earlier today Martha had told him about the *thing* – the awful, senseless thing which unbeknownst to him had so shocked Noa when she had heard it at her window.

'There is nothing we can do,' she had said, when Raffy raged at her that they had to stop it.

Bea could have stopped it, if they'd given her a chance. Raffy knew she could have. But now on top of the awful thing, there was this new terrible betrayal.

In all his life, Raffy had never known such treachery.

And he didn't see how even Bea could get round it.

'Here she is!' said Martha.

Raffy craned his neck to look and there was Bea, walking beside a uniformed official, her hair a fiery halo in the gloom of the station hall, her hand raised in a wave ... Martha hurried towards her. Raffy followed, dragging his feet.

How would she take the news?

She was standing with her back to him, bouncing up and down in an impatient gesture he knew well, while Martha signed some papers. She turned towards him and beamed, completely unrepentant about the havoc she had caused, and ran to hug him.

Raffy's heart lurched. He should tell her now. But she had already let him go as Martha joined them, was hitching up her rucksack and looking round the station. 'Come on, let's go!' she said, and Martha, looking like she was about to cry again, explained.

They weren't going to Ravenwood. Alex and Ingrid were flying back to London from Venice. Martha was to keep Bea in town until they arrived.

Bea said nothing. She just stood stock-still and stared, and Raffy knew exactly what she was thinking.

Everything she had done to get here, for this! To be delivered back to the people she had run from!

He could have wept. A kid. That's what she was. Not a Valkyrie or a hero, just a kid like him, in a world of problems made by grown-ups where being a kid didn't amount to anything.

'Let's go,' said Martha, as gently as she could.

Side by side, not touching or talking, Bea and Raffy followed her towards Kings Cross Underground station, where they waited by the machines for Martha to buy Bea's ticket.

Raffy swallowed. He had to tell Bea about the *thing*, but he didn't know how. Instead, he asked, 'Bea, what were you going to do, if you had got back to Ravenwood? How were you going to stop Leo from selling? That *is* what you were trying to do, isn't it?'

'I was just going to talk to him.' Bea sighed. 'I thought maybe he'd listen to me.'

'Oh.' Raffy was a little disappointed. 'Do you think he would? He didn't listen to Mum.'

'He'd listen to *me*,' grumbled Bea. 'I just need to get him face to face.'

Raffy squirmed and stared at his feet.

'There's something else you need to know,' he said.

And, still hoping she would work an impossible miracle to save them, he told her the awful thing.

'Ant's going to cut down Ygg.'

'What?' Bea stopped walking and whipped round to face him. 'When?'

'Someone's coming tomorrow morning at nine o'clock.'

'But how? Ravenwood isn't even his yet!'

Raffy shrugged miserably. 'Ant says Ygg's in the way. Apparently he knows a tree man, and he's free tomorrow, and Jack says it's fine to go ahead.'

'And Leo's ok with this?' Bea was outraged.

'Mum says it was the last straw for Leo, whatever that means. She says he's given up. He told her, Ant'll cut down Ygg sooner or later, so what difference does it make?'

'Oh,' said Bea.

Raffy knew then that Martha was right, and that there really was nothing they could do. Bea's *oh* was not a determined *oh* – the *oh* of a girl who can do anything. The sort of *oh* that means *oh, we'll see about that!* or *oh, they are, are they! More* the sort which, spoken very quietly, means *it's over*.

'Where are we going now?' she asked.

'To my grandmother's.'

'Oh yes,' said Bea wanly. 'Your grandmother. I forgot about her.'

'I'll tell you everything on the tube.'

Bea nodded, too tired for more questions. They walked down a flight of steps to their platform, where they stood side by side looking at the tracks.

Over, thought Raffy.

Their lovely life. Eleven years together.

Over, over, over.

On the track, something darted, then stopped. Raffy frowned. Had he imagined it? No, there it was again. Something tiny, the exact dusty brown as the space between the rails. He leaned forward. A mouse! Raffy grunted, his nature enthusiast's instinct prickling through his sadness. A tiny mouse, scurrying beside the tracks . . . left, then right, then straight up the wall in front of them and into a hole where it disappeared.

The memory came from nowhere and felt like a punch. Noa's drawing, when she first came to Ravenwood. Raffy as a mouse. What had he said to Bea, when she was so cross about it?

People think mice are all timid, but they're actually really brave.

He looked again at Bea, standing exhausted beside him. Why did he think she was the one who had to save them? What if *he* could be brave too? What if *he* could do something as daring, as outrageous, as Bea had?

'Bea,' he whispered. 'How did you do it? When you left Venice, how did you get the train without anyone stopping you?'

'I just jumped,' Bea said. 'It was surprisingly easy, compared with trying to convince grown-ups to care.'

'Right,' said Raffy.

A distant rumble getting closer, a blast of hot stale air, a screech of brakes. Their train thundered into the station. The passengers on the platform surged forward.

'Stay close now!' Martha ordered.

Right behind Martha, Bea and Raffy advanced with the crowd towards the train doors. Closer, closer ... Martha stepped on board, using her arms to carve a space for the children.

Raffy stopped, dropped to the ground. Grabbed the hem of Bea's dress to stop her moving forward.

'My ticket!'

More passengers crammed into the train after Martha.

'Leave it!' she shouted. 'Raffy, just get on!'

She tried to fight the tide to get to him, but there were too many people. With a series of beeps, the doors slid shut.

'Run!' Raffy yelled.

Hand in hand, Raffy and Bea sprinted back up the steps and away from the Underground, laughing so much it hurt.

'Two children,' Martha garbled to two London Transport Police officers, after she had fought her way off her train at the next stop and – repeatedly – pressed the emergency button on the platform. 'A small brown boy in a grey hoodie, a red-haired white girl in a blue one. They've run away, and I don't know what to do.'

One of the police officers asked, did she have any idea where the children might be running to?

Martha said, 'I think they might be going home.'

The police officer raised two perfectly pencilled eyebrows.

'I know that sounds mad,' said Martha, and started to cry again.

The police officer, who didn't have children but did have a mum who worried, said no, not mad, and asked what the children were running *from*. Martha, sniffing loudly and accepting a tissue from the officer's colleague, said they were running from Bea's parents, who wanted to separate them, even though they had been raised together since babies, and now they had some hopeless plan to save their beloved home from being destroyed, or not destroyed exactly but having its soul ripped out, starting with a beautiful tree, and the police officer (her name was Eloïse) said that was a shame.

Martha, now sobbing, said that yes it was, and she didn't know what she was going to do next, where to live or anything because the last eleven years had been the happiest of her life and she was sorry to be crying but she hadn't slept last night on account of Bea running away from Venice. That did sound stressful, said Eloïse, but also Bea sounded like a very enterprising young person so maybe Martha shouldn't worry too much and also people shouldn't go around ripping out trees, not in this day and age. At which point her colleague stepped in and asked, how old were the children and where exactly was this tree, and how did Martha think they were planning to get to it?

By the time all the relevant phone calls had been made to find them, Bea and Raffy were long gone. The landslide had been cleared, and the train was fast. The police finally picked them up when it stopped at Doncaster, by which point they were so close to Ravenwood there was no point taking them back to London. They were brought home in a squad car, as the first stars pierced the twilight sky.

CHAPTER TWENTY-FIVE

When she heard Bea and Raffy come in, Noa's first impulse was to run out of her room to greet them. She wanted to know about everything – their journey, Elva, their plans! But at the top of the stairs she stopped. Directly beneath her in the hall, his shoulders racked with sobs, Leo stood with his arms around both children, crushing them to his chest in a gesture so full of raw emotion Noa instinctively knew it was not for her.

After a minute or so, Leo let the children go. Raffy murmured something Noa couldn't hear, and Leo with a hoarse bark of laughter began to usher him along the corridor towards the kitchen. Bea looked up before following them, and her face lit up when she saw Noa.

'There you are!' she shouted. 'Come down!'

But still Noa hung back. Despite everything that had happened between Bea and her – all those messages, the connection with Elva – she still felt unsure of herself. *I don't understand what happened*, Bea had written about the fire, and Noa had got the impression she was on her side. But what if she was wrong? What if, under her apparent friendliness, Bea blamed Noa for all that had happened? And what about Raffy? There had been no contact between him and Noa since he went away. Did *he* agree with Bea, or did he blame Noa for the fire? The thought made her itch with shame.

'Leo's making hot chocolate!' Bea's hair and clothes were a mess and her face was pale with exhaustion, but she was clearly still exhilarated from her adventure. 'Come down! There are mini marshmallows!'

Noa squared her shoulders. If Bea and Raffy were brave enough to run away, surely she could find the courage to go downstairs. It was pointless to try and hide, anyway. She was going to face them all sooner or later.

By the time she reached the kitchen, however, nobody was concerned about her at all. Leo's first flush of relief had given way to recriminations. He was in full scolding mode, and Bea and Raffy were defending themselves.

'I just can't believe you could be so selfish, Bea!' Leo was saying, as Noa came in. 'Running away! Worrying everyone sick! The pair of you, tricking Martha after all she's been through! As for involving Noa's sister, for God's sake!'

'Elva was glad to help me!' Bea cried indignantly. 'Wasn't she, Noa?'

Noa, remembering Leo's outrage at the part she had played in Bea's escape, cringed and nodded at the same time, wishing that she could disappear.

'And anyway,' Bea went on, 'I only did it because you ...'

'Don't you dare say you did it because of me, Bea! Don't you dare say it was my fault!'

'But it was,' said Raffy stoutly, righteous anger making him forgo his usual role of peacekeeper.

'Don't you start, Raffy!'

'But it's true!' cried Bea. 'You agreed to sell

Ravenwood! I came back to beg you not to! And now Ygg – *Ygg*, Leo. Ygg!'

Leo gave a shout of exasperation. 'Do you not think you could have begged me over the phone instead of sending yours to flipping Naples?'

'I tried to call but you didn't answer!'

'What, so you just thought you would *stow away across half of Europe* instead?'

'I *had* to get away. I had to! You can't just sell Ravenwood without asking me! And you can't just give me back to my parents like I'm some sort of, some sort of…'

'Library book,' said Raffy.

'*Library book?*' cried Leo.

'You *can't* let them cut down Ygg!' Bea clung to her uncle's arm. 'Leo, it's *Ygg*! It's like … the soul of Ravenwood!Call Uncle Jack now and tell him you've changed your mind. Call him, Leo!'

Leo glared at her, then groaned and buried his hands in his hair.

'Bea, I can't discuss this. I know it's horrible. Believe me, nobody hates this more than I do. And I'm sorry, more sorry than I can ever say, because living here at Ravenwood with you and Raffy and Martha has been the joy of my life. If there was something I could do, I would. But your dad and Jack haven't left me any choice.'

His expression as he held his hands out towards Bea and Raffy was so desperate Noa couldn't bear to look.

Bea showed no such compassion.

'You're not even trying,' she snorted.

Leo flinched. 'That's not fair!'

'Well, you're not,' Bea went on mercilessly. 'Ever since we were little, you've told us there's always a choice. Maybe not a *nice* choice, but *a* choice. Well, *I* chose to run away to stop you, and so did Raffy. Now *you* could choose to stop this.'

'For the love of everything I care about, Bea, how can I make you understand *I can't afford to buy Ravenwood from my brothers*. I've crunched the numbers, I've tried to raise a mortgage – there just isn't enough money.'

'Oh, *money*,' said Bea scornfully. She walked towards the door. 'I don't want hot chocolate after all,' she announced, by way of a parting shot. 'I would only *choke* on it.'

She stomped away past Noa towards the stairs. Raffy, after a quick backward glance at Leo which was half pity, half resentment, went after her.

Noa, feeling increasingly uncertain, followed them up to Bea's room, where Bea threw her arms around her in a quick, angry hug.

'Can you believe Leo?' Bea cried. 'After all we did to get here, he won't even listen to us! I was sure we could get him to change his mind, but he's so stubborn!'

Noa hugged her back then sat on the floor, not quite meeting Raffy's eye.

'What are you going to do now?' she asked.

'Fight!' said Bea. 'Me and Raffy made a plan on the train. Can we use your phone to call your sister? We need her to tell us exactly what to do.'

All through the next hour, as they spoke to Elva, used Noa's phone to research websites she recommended, made notes, planned and plotted, nobody mentioned the fire or Noa's part in it. It was possible Bea and Raffy weren't thinking about it, but for Noa, the less they said, the more the subject grew, until it was impossible to focus on anything else.

Just before midnight, Bea declared they were ready.

'We'd better try and sleep a bit now,' she yawned. 'We've got to be up again in a few hours to get everything done before Jack gets back at nine.'

But Noa couldn't go to bed now, not feeling like this. If she did, without telling them what she had to say, there would be more nightmares, and they would go on, and on, and she would never sleep again. She might die of shame and embarrassment saying it, but she cleared her throat anyway.

'There's just one thing.'

Bea stifled another yawn. Raffy, seeing Noa blush looked alarmed.

Noa wiped her hands on her shorts. 'I just want to say I'm sorry. You know, about the fire. Like I said before, I was so sure I had put the lantern away, but there's no other explanation, and I – well, I just feel so bad about it and I hope you can forgive me.'

She hung her head as she waited for their answer.

Bea scrunched up her face as she thought about what to say. Somehow, it had felt easier to dismiss the story of the lantern when she was far away. Now that Noa stood before her full of remorse, the idea that she had accidentally started the fire was harder to ignore. But she remembered then what she had promised herself at the Gare du Nord – that she would pay back all the people who had helped her. Noa had helped her a *lot*. And she wanted to be fair.

'I'll be honest,' she said at last. 'At first when you messaged after the fire I was so upset about Skid I almost didn't answer. And I still don't understand how it started. But what I do know is that if it was the lantern, you didn't do it on purpose, and I know how awful you must be feeling because I would be devastated if it were me. And I don't really know about forgiving – I mean, I don't know if you *need* to forgive people for things they do by accident – but if it means still being friends in spite of bad things that happen, then I forgive you. And so does Raffy, don't you, Raffy?'

Raffy squirmed. Noa flushed.

'Raffy!' Bea was appalled. 'Tell Noa you forgive her!'

But Raffy didn't know *what* to say. He didn't know what he *thought*. Noa looked so miserable ...

The old Raffy would have done anything to spare her feelings, but this new Raffy he was becoming – the Raffy who told his mother she wasn't being fair and kicked sofas and ran away on trains – needed to tell the truth.

'The thing is,' he said cautiously, 'the fire didn't exactly help.'

'Well, of course it didn't *help!*' scoffed Bea. She put her arm around Noa. 'That's not the point.'

Raffy frowned. He loved Bea so much, but he did wish sometimes she would just let him speak.

'I do know, though, that you would never have done it on purpose,' he went on. 'Because you loved Skid, and also you're not that sort of person. So of course I forgive you and want to be friends. And I think … well, I just think that now we should forget about Skid and concentrate on saving Ygg and Ravenwood.' He gazed at her anxiously. 'Does that make you feel better?'

Noa nodded. She would have preferred them to say they didn't believe she had started the fire, but it would do.

For now.

'Also,' said Raffy, keen to move on from this uncomfortable subject, 'I have an idea.'

Bea sighed. '*Please* can we just go to bed? Honestly, I'm so tired I might actually be sick.'

'Let's sleep in the tree house!' said Raffy, and Noa couldn't help it, her heart gave a little leap and she actually clapped her hands.

'The tree house?' Bea looked longingly at her bed, but they could both see that she was tempted.

'It's so beautiful, Bea,' Raffy said. 'Isn't it, Noa? It's exactly how I said it was going to be. And I don't think Ygg should be alone tonight. Not if it's the last one.'

'It's not Ygg's last night,' said Bea firmly.

'Even so,' said Raffy. 'Let's go there, now, the three of us.'

Out they went carrying their bedclothes, into the shadowy garden, and followed the moon's path to the old ash tree.

For a minute or so, the three children stayed still on the platform and listened. Then, with no need for words, they went into the tree house where, after Bea had admired every inch of the cabin, they climbed on to the bunks.

There was so much they could have said to each other. *Do you remember when Leo first brought us up here? The first time we came up alone? Do you remember the stories Martha read us, the time the wood pigeon pooed on your head, the robin who used to share our picnic, the squirrel with the scars which had been in a fight, when the nuthatch came? Noa, do you remember our breakfast picnic?* They could have talked of Bea's journey – only last night! – of Paris – only today! – of London and Raffy's grandmother and his grandfather's paintings.

Noa could have told them about the fire, how scared she had been. Her fruitless search through the ashes for proof it wasn't her fault.

They could have talked about tomorrow.

But they didn't.

Moonlight streamed through the window, throwing the shadows of leaves and branches across the floor.

Bea wanted to say that for all the beautiful things she had seen since going away, Venice, the *Carolina*, the Adriatic coastline, nothing compared to this, the shadows cast by the moon on the bare wooden floor in Ygg.

But the others were already asleep.

Bea stayed awake a few minutes longer, then she too drifted off.

Outside, the owl screeched as it flew through the woods, the prey of the hunting fox cried out. Leaves rustled, branches creaked. In the distance, the sea pulled in and out.

The children in the tree house slept on.

The old tree watched over them all.

CHAPTER TWENTY-SIX

Long before daybreak, three shadows crept down from the tree house towards the biggest of the Ravenwood barns. Shortly afterwards, two emerged again, pushing bicycles. At the raven gate, they climbed on and sped silently away down the hill.

At the furthest end of the village, in one of the new bungalows, Nick was already making tea. He had been a late sleeper when his wife was alive, and she the early riser. 'It's like the world's a gift, every single day,' she used to tell him, and turned out she was right. It was the loneliness that got him since she was gone. The endless summer days, the long winter nights. They'd never talked much, him and Nell.

Never had to, because they each always knew what the other was thinking. Nick didn't have friends, as such. Nell had been the one to get on with people, he was too shy. If it hadn't been for Ravenwood, these last years, he didn't know how he would have coped. But now that was going too, and though Nick wasn't one for being dramatic, it felt like his heart was breaking all over again. As for the plans for Yggdrasil, they made his blood boil. To cut down an ancient, perfectly healthy ash, when all over the country specimens were succumbing to disease! It was madness.

Worse than madness – it was murder.

He tried not to think about the tree house, how it had felt to build the cabin with Raffy and Noa and Leo, giving new life to dead beech wood. The hours spent working on it had been the happiest since Nell's passing.

The ring of his doorbell made him jump. Shuffling into the hallway in his slippers, he recognised Raffy's small frame through the frosted glass of the front door, and his poor hurt heart quickened like it already knew something his head didn't.

'Give me a few minutes to dress,' he said, after Raffy had spoken. 'Then I'll be on my way.'

Up and down the village street, throwing pebbles at closed windows, calling softly at open ones, Bea and Raffy woke the people they knew would help.

'What is it?' sleepy voices whispered.

'It's about Ravenwood,' they replied, and in hushed tones explained what they needed to do to save Ygg and to stop Leo selling.

'You mean, like fight?' they asked.

'Exactly,' they replied.

In the pre-dawn darkness, from cottages and flats, new-builds and ancient dwellings, they came – children who had known Ravenwood all their lives, the elderly who had found solace there helping in the garden, members of the Nature Society who had delighted in its abundance.

Out of the shadows, an army grew.

CHAPTER TWENTY-SEVEN

Up at Ravenwood, Noa was exploring the barns.

'Look for anything useful.' That's what Elva had told them on the phone last night. 'You'd be surprised what you can do with what you think is junk. You've just got to try and look at it differently.'

Noa, standing at the entrance of the largest barn, sweeping her phone torch across its contents, tried not to feel defeated. There was a *lot* of junk here and no apparent order to it. In an old cattle manger, she found a sack of charcoal. In another, pots of old paint, bottles of turpentine, poorly cleaned brushes dried into clumps. What was she supposed to do with these?

She moved on.

In another section of the barn, beside a towering woodpile, she found old bicycles stacked against each other, ancient and rusting – far too old to be Bea's and Raffy's, she realised. They must have belonged to Leo and his brothers. Beyond them, stacked against the wall, she found several mildewed mattresses. Beside them, a travelling trunk filled with old curtains covered in mouse droppings and most definitely nibbled ... In a corner, a bundle of willow sticks, presumably for gardening, a ball of string, a coil of rope, a stack of cardboard boxes.

Noa, having completed her tour of the barn, returned to the first cattle manger and stared at it.

Charcoal! How could you look at charcoal differently? Charcoal was just charcoal. You used it for barbecues ... and to draw things.

Noa's pulse began to race as she remembered a photograph of Elva after she was arrested, her face streaked with the paint she had used to draw the polar bear on the side of the building. War paint, she had called it, which had made Mum roll her eyes.

Well, if Elva had done it . . .

Noa picked up a piece of charcoal and rubbed it in a single line across her face, then looked at herself in her phone's camera.

A good look, she decided. Powerful. She pocketed the charcoal and moved on.

Something was unlocked now. Everywhere Noa looked she saw how things could be useful. Most of the paint in the pots had formed crusts, but she found one of red and one of green which, when stirred with a stick, proved fresh enough to work. She whacked the brushes against the wall to get rid of dust. A few were still serviceable. She picked up the pots, put the brushes in her pockets, left them by the door then went back to carry on her search.

The old mattresses, the coil of rope, the chain, the bicycle locks. The willow sticks! Noa thought of uses for them all, and as she dragged them to the entrance of the barn she felt more and more elated.

She had a purpose again, just as she had building the tree house with Nick and the others. No longer the girl who had started the fire, but the girl who was putting it right.

The sky was beginning to lighten when Raffy crept in.

'Wow!' he said, admiring Noa's hoard, then, 'Wow!' again, looking at her coal-streaked face.

Noa glowed with pride.

'I thought we could use these as banners,' she said, showing him the curtains. 'There's paint, and brushes. I thought we could hang them from the tree house.' She danced around the pile, while Raffy spun slowly from one item to the next, grinning as he took it all in. 'And we can use the cardboard from the boxes to make placards, and tie them on the willow sticks with string. The mattresses are just to put around the tree for people to sit on, and there's rope to tie people together so they can't be moved – that's what Elva and her friends did once . . .'

'Look at everything Noa found!' Raffy whispered, as Bea came in.

'Amazing!' Bea, like the others, couldn't keep still, bouncing on the balls of her feet as she inspected her finds.

'And look at her face!' said Raffy.

Noa, feeling bold, picked up a piece of charcoal.

'Hold still,' she told Bea.

'How do I look?' Bea asked with a grin when Noa had drawn a line across her face.

'Fierce!' said Raffy, clapping his hands.

Dizzy with excitement, he took the charcoal and drew it across his face.

'How's that?' he asked.

'Terrifying!' said Bea.

'We should make another pact,' said Raffy. 'Like we did in Ygg before you went away.'

Serious suddenly, he held out his right hand.

'For Ygg!' he said. 'May we not rest until we win!'

First Bea, then Noa put their right hands over his. Once again, as she had with that other pact over a week ago in Yggdrasil, and despite the solemnity of the situation, Noa felt a stab of joy.

But then . . .

'Let's get all this out to Ygg,' said Bea. 'People are starting to arrive.'

Heavily laden, they crossed the meadow to

Yggdrasil, where a dozen children were milling in barely contained silence beneath the great ash.

'Everyone, this is Noa,' said Bea – and Noa's newly found confidence collapsed.

A dozen heads turned, a dozen pairs of eyes looked. Friendly enough, but Noa distinctly heard a small girl in stripy dungarees ask an older boy in shorts, 'Is that the girl who started the fire?'

'Shh,' said the boy. 'I heard she feels really bad.'

That was all, but it was enough.

All through the next hour, Noa kept going. Directed the recruits as they ferried back and forth across the meadow to bring all the stuff over from the barn, showed them the paint to use for signs and banners, helped to spread the mattresses around the bottom of the tree. When the older people began to arrive in their cars – Nick, Magda and other members of the Nature Society, Elena the librarian, the volunteers from the village shop – she was polite and explained what they were to do too. But when everything was in place, Noa went quietly over to where Bea was securing a banner to a willow stick with string, and said, 'I can't do it.'

'Do what?' asked Bea, frowning in concentration.

'Be part of the fight.'

'What?' Bea stopped mid knot and stared at her in disbelief. 'Noa, you *are* part of the fight. We can't do it without you!'

'Yes, you can.' Noa waved towards the meadow where about thirty people ranging in ages from early primary to post-retirement were getting into their battle positions. 'You've got all of them.'

'But it's not the same!' Bea seized Noa's hands. '*Please* stay, Noa! You've been part of this since the beginning! What about our pact? This isn't because of the fire, is it? You know nobody believes it was your fault!'

'But that's where you're wrong,' said Noa. 'People do. Even you and Raffy. I know you said you forgive me, but you still think it happened because of something I did. It *is* my fault. I've done all I can to put it right but I ... I can't stay here, fighting alongside people who know Ygg might die because of something I started.'

Bea wanted to disagree, but at that moment a cry went up from Yggdrasil where Raffy stood on the roof of the tree house, a pair of binoculars trained on the lane.

'Van coming!' he shouted, voice high with trepidation. 'It's the tree man!'

Noa softly disengaged her hands from Bea's. 'Good luck.'

'But Noa ... Noa, wait! Where will you go?'

'He's reached the top of the hill!' Raffy shrieked. 'Everyone, get ready!'

Bea turned to look over the gate towards the lane. By the time she turned back, Noa had gone.

Where else would you go, on the day a tree was scheduled to die? Noa ran to the woods.

Is that the girl who started the fire?

The words echoed through her head as her feet pounded the ground.

The girl who started the fire ...

Yes, that was her, and it was what she would always be.

She reached the pond, sat down on the old pontoon, and drew her knees up to her chest.

Raffy had told her once about the pond's magic

properties. 'It shows you exactly what you want,' he had said.

But what *did* she want?

For Ygg to be saved, she told herself. For Ravenwood not to be sold. For the fire never to have happened.

All of these things, she wanted. But what she saw in her mind's eye, as she stared into the pond's dark water, was a little girl with light brown skin and her hair in pigtails, holding hands with her mother and father, happy, before it all went wrong.

CHAPTER TWENTY-EIGHT

The tree man's full name was Colin Fanshawe, and really the only thing he knew about trees was how to cut them down. This he would do cheerfully for anyone who paid him, and the more they paid him, the more cheerful he became. Since Ant Rainer was paying him a lot, with the promise of more work in the months to come, when Colin turned on to the Ravenwood lane just before nine o'clock he was in an excellent mood. Bouncing up the hill in his van, he even began to whistle. But as the raven gate came into view, the tune died on his lips.

'Huh?'

Cars. So many of them.

The elderly inhabitants of Ashby-under-Raven tried to share transport as a general rule to save on fuel, but today they had brought as many vehicles as possible and parked them across the lane in a makeshift barricade.

Colin swore and leaned on the van's horn.

No one came.

He leaned more heavily and for longer.

Beyond the cars, on the other side of the gate, a red-haired girl with two black stripes across her face appeared, carrying some sort of sign.

Colin squinted.

SAVE OUR TREE!

More children began to appear, also with curiously smeared faces, and more signs.

RAVENWOOD FOREVER!

HANDS OFF YGG!

'Huh?' repeated Colin. He scratched his head. What should he do?

Reason suggested that he should leave and come again another day, when the path was not blocked by cars and children waving placards.

But then, there was the money.

He was still weighing up his options when Ant and Jack arrived.

'What's all this?' Jack shouted, as he strode towards Colin.

Colin pointed towards the gate, where a third sign had appeared, instructing him to STOP DISTROYING NATURE.

Jack's expression darkened.

'I could come back tomorrow,' Colin offered.

'Oh no, you won't.'

Jack began to thread his way through the tightly packed cars.

'I don't mind,' said Colin.

'Hang about a bit longer, mate.' Ant grinned to hide his irritation. 'Jack'll sort this out.'

'Too right I will.' Jack swore as a bramble snagged his shirt. There was the sound of ripping cotton as he yanked it away. 'I know exactly who's behind this, and I'm going to stop them!'

CHAPTER TWENTY-NINE

'They're coming!' yelled Bea. 'Everyone, to your posts!'

What a sight it was at Ravenwood! While the party at the gate had been welcoming Colin, the older protestors had secured their positions on the mattresses at the foot of Yggdrasil, seated in a circle around the trunk, the rope from the barn looped around their bodies. Magda from the Nature Society had brought a hand drum, and was leading them all in song. Above them, the children who had not been at the gate were already perched in the branches of Yggdrasil. A huge banner hung from the tree house, exactly as Noa had imagined it, hastily painted with the slogan VICTORY WILL BE OURS!

As Jack, Ant and Colin came towards the raven gate, the young protestors on the ground sprinted back to Yggdrasil, abandoned their placards and scrambled for the rope ladder. Bea went last, pausing to admire the battlefield with a triumphant smile. It was magnificent. And it was going to work! All they needed now was Leo to see how much support he had, and he would finally make the right choice.

She just knew he would.

'Bea, hurry!' yelled Raffy.

She glanced over her shoulder. Jack was running towards her, and he did not look like he thought any of this was magnificent at all. She skimmed up the rope ladder to the tree house's platform, Raffy pulling it up behind her just as Jack's hand was about to close on it.

From the branches above the tree house, whoops and cheers rang out.

'Beatrice Pembury, come down this instant!' Jack shouted.

From the tree house roof, Raffy handed down a loudspeaker, a relic from days past when the meadow at Ravenwood was a lawn used for ad-hoc tennis matches. Bea took a few seconds to catch her breath, then raised it to her mouth.

'NO!'

Even louder whoops and cheers from the branches above. Bea grinned. It was amazing how powerful people shouting could make you feel, if they were on your side.

'Look, kid.' Ant had joined Jack at the foot of Yggdrasil and held out his hands, like he wanted to make friends. 'I get that this is tough, and believe me if it wasn't necessary, I wouldn't do it. But the tree's in the way.'

'In the way of what?' shouted Bea.

'I need this space for a car park,' Ant said. 'For my building machinery.'

'A CAR PARK?' jeered Bea into the loudspeaker. 'FOR YOUR BUILDING MACHINERY????'

Boos from the branches. Hisses and foot stamping from the ground. Banging from Magda's drum.

Ant ignored them.

'Listen to me,' he said. 'I promise I'll plant other trees. Heaps of trees, to replace this one. And, you know ...' He glanced at the STOP DISTROYING

NATURE placard now being held by Nick and Magda. 'To help the planet.'

'Tell him it takes forty years for a tree like Ygg to start storing carbon,' shouted Raffy. 'Ask him about all the other trees he's planning to chop down in the woods to make room for his stupid cabins. Tell him about the biodiversity crisis and all the animals and birds that live in Ygg. Idiot!'

'You do know I can hear you, don't you?' said Ant. 'Look, kids, what is it you want? Apart from saving this tree?'

Bea's friend Maisie, from higher up, yelled something rude about why didn't Ant go away and leave Ravenwood alone.

'That's not going to happen,' Ant said calmly. 'My lawyers are drawing up papers as we speak. Believe me, I understand. I used to go on marches, but here's what I've learned: they don't work. Come on down and let's talk about this.'

'Don't listen to him!' shouted the librarian. 'He's playing with your mind.'

Bea glared at Ant. 'I'm not coming down until you go away!'

Ant shrugged. 'And I'm not going away.'

Apparently, they had reached a stalemate.

And the only man who could break it was nowhere to be seen.

Down at the cove, Leo lay on his back on the sun-warmed boulders, looking at the sky through half-closed eyes and trying hard not to think.

He had weakened and his brothers had won. That didn't mean he had to stay and watch Yggdrasil die. He had come down here at dawn with a flask of coffee, just as his mother used to do when she couldn't sleep. Watched the sunrise, had a swim and now here he was. Enjoying the sun.

The thing was not to get emotional but be completely practical instead. There would be money from the sale. He and Martha could buy another house. Not a big house – Ant had driven a hard bargain. Ravenwood's quirks, its antique electrical system, its leaking roof had all driven the price down – but a house nonetheless. Millions of people around the world didn't have houses. *Billions*. He had no right to complain.

Oh, but Bea . . .

The family they had created over these eleven years, the four of them, the home they had made, the paradise Ravenwood had become . . .

His gut twisted as he thought about the moment the phone call came from Alex to tell him Bea had gone missing. God, he'd been so worried. Like the bottom had fallen out of his world.

So what was he doing here, he thought suddenly – on this beach, pretending it was any other day, leaving Bea and Raffy and Noa alone while this terrible thing took place at Ravenwood?

What sort of person did that make him?

A completely rubbish one, that was what. The least he could do was be there with them when Ygg fell. And maybe later they could go out, to another beach perhaps. But then he remembered that Alex and Ingrid would be on their way now, with poor Martha who had waited in London last night in case the children were brought back there. Well, maybe they could come too. If Bea was going to live with her parents, he had better keep on good terms with them, however much he hated them right now.

With an effort, he got to his feet and pulled on his clothes, then began to make his way back towards the cliff.

He had no idea what was waiting for him.

CHAPTER THIRTY

Up in Yggdrasil, Bea refused to be disheartened by Leo's continued absence, and was rallying the protest with chants rehearsed last night in her bedroom over YouTube videos on Noa's phone.

'WHAT DO WE WANT?' she shouted into the loudspeaker.

'TO SAVE OUR TREE!' the protestors shouted back.

'WHEN DO WE WANT IT?'

'NOW!'

'WHOSE TREE IS IT?' shouted Bea, warming to her task.

'OUR TREE!'

'WHOSE BIRDS?'

'OUR BIRDS!'

'WHOSE PLANET?'

'OUR PLANET!'

Bea's heart was ballooning. How could anyone fail to be moved by so much caring, so much passion, so much *love*? Surely anyone who cared about the world would join their cause! Jack, who had stepped away from the tree a few minutes ago to make a phone call, was striding back towards Ygg with an air of purpose. She thought back to the evening when he had spoken so beautifully about his garden in Costa Rica. Surely now even he might change his mind? He came to stand beneath the tree house and looked up. Bea interrupted her chanting and gazed down at him hopefully.

'Bea,' he said, and as soon as he opened his mouth she knew he hadn't had a miraculous change of heart. 'I have been talking to your parents. They're almost here. Come on, stop this. Don't you think you've caused them enough trouble?'

Her parents! Bea swallowed. Raffy, balancing precariously on the pitched roof, stifled a curse. Even now, after all that had happened. Even now, she still feared her parents' disapproval! He thought back to Kings Cross, to the mouse he had seen between the tracks of the Underground. Be brave, he thought. Brave like a little mouse who lives among thundering trains. Bea wasn't the only one who could be a leader, he knew that now! And he might not have a loudspeaker, but he did have a voice.

He let go of the branch that was supporting him and cupped his hands around his mouth.

'ARE WE SCARED OF PARENTS?'

'NO!'

'NO WHAT?'

'WE'RE NOT SCARED OF OUR PARENTS!'

It was working. Raffy grinned as Bea raised the loudspeaker once more to her mouth.

'WHOSE PLANET?' she cried.

'OUR PLANET!'

Minutes later, Maisie shouted that a car was coming up the lane, that it had stopped at the end of the traffic barricade, that Bea's parents and Martha were getting out . . .

'There's an older lady with them.'

'What?'

Raffy shifted position to get a better view. There, squeezing and shuffling between the cars, looking very tiny and very neat and very curious, was his grandmother.

But there was no time for questions. Alex, in a flying rage, was marching ahead of the three women straight towards Yggdrasil.

'You should be ashamed of yourselves!' he seethed at the chanting grown-ups sitting round the base of the trunk. 'Encouraging children! What if someone gets hurt? And you –' glaring up at Bea – 'haven't you worried your mother enough?'

On the ground, the older protestors shifted uncomfortably and wondered if Alex did have a point about safety. In the tree, the chanting faltered. It was easy to defy parents when parents weren't there. Harder when one was right in front of you, shouting.

Doubt bubbled in Bea's throat. She tried to push it down, to think of Venice, the way her parents had announced she was to live with them without consulting her, the holiday intended to test her. She glanced up at Raffy, who glared back fiercely. At Martha, on whose face she thought she distinguished a flicker of pride. *They* never tested her, she reminded herself. *They* loved her without question. Her parents might not like what she was doing, but this was who she was.

Up came the loudspeaker again, and as she began to chant Bea looked her father straight in the eye.

'WHOSE TREES?'

Rallied by her cry, all of the protestors responded as one.

'OUR TREES!'

'WHOSE HOME?'

'OUR HOME!'

'WHOSE PLANET?'

'OUR PLANET!'

Alex turned to Martha. 'You tell them,' he ordered. 'Explain that they are being absurd.'

To his intense irritation, Martha grinned.

'Oh, I don't think so, Alex,' she murmured. 'I don't believe they're being absurd at all.'

Alex exploded. 'That is *exactly* the sort of comment that makes me not want my daughter to live with you! Tell those children to come down *now*!'

Martha flinched, but still did not do as he asked. Grandma pressed her lips together. Martha had told her not to come this morning. It was a long journey, she had said, and an early start. Her presence was not necessary. But Grandma had come anyway. She had disapproved of Ingrid and Alex from the moment she heard about the sale of Ravenwood and their plans for Bea's future. She might have had differences with her own daughter, but there was no way she was letting Martha travel alone for hours with the people who were about to render her homeless. Nor now was she about to let this man be rude to her.

'It seems to me,' she said acidly, 'that if your daughter is anything like my grandson, Martha has done a rather good job of raising her.'

'Thank you, Mum.' Martha flushed, pleased and astonished by the unexpected praise.

'You're welcome, dear.' Grandma curled her lip at Alex, in a gesture as unmissable as it was barely visible, then took her daughter's arm. 'Now, it's been a long drive and I would like to use the bathroom. Perhaps you could show me the way?'

Alex watched them go with a huff of exasperation, then touched Ingrid's arm.

'Darling, you talk to Bea,' he said. 'Get her to see sense. She'll listen to you.'

But Ingrid was staring at Bea and did not answer.

'Ingrid!'

She turned to him with shining eyes.

'*Look* at her, Alex!'

'I *am* looking at her,' he replied. 'And I am not pleased.'

'No, *really* look at her. She's ...' Ingrid searched for the right word. 'She's incredible.' She laid her hand on Alex's arm. 'I'm sorry, dear. But really, that beautiful tree ...'

And before everyone's astonished gaze, Ingrid left her husband's side and walked to Yggdrasil, where she sat down on the mattress between Nick and Magda.

A resounding cheer went up. Alex flushed. Magda began to sing. From the far edge of the meadow, on their way into the house, Martha and Grandma watched.

'Well!' said Grandma.

Martha's lips twitched.

One by one, the protestors joined in the singing. Ingrid craned round to look up at her astonished daughter and waved shyly.

Bea, her mouth hanging open, waved back.

Gently, Raffy leaned down to prise the loudspeaker from her and raised it to his mouth.

'WHOOOSE TREE?'

The chanting resumed, louder than before.

They so very nearly won the fight.

Leo heard it before he saw it, his ear catching the sound of chanting as he came through the meadow. He stopped, confused. Then, as hope began to rise, he broke into a run, only stopping when the full beauty of what was happening came into view. All these people! The placards, the banners! Yggdrasil full of chanting children, Raffy bellowing through a loudspeaker, his wonderful niece beside him, and was that *Ingrid* sitting on the ground between Nick and Magda?

If you had told Leo this morning that today he would laugh, he wouldn't have believed you, but laugh he did.

On the ground, in the tree house, in the branches of Yggdrasil, the protestors saw the glow on Leo's face and for a heady few seconds believed that victory was theirs. Buoyed by their support, now was the moment when Leo would change his mind and refuse to sell Ravenwood, when Yggdrasil was saved! Softly at first, then louder and louder, a rumbling cheer went up as they waited for him to speak.

But a battle is never over till it's over.

One person (quite literally) brought it all crashing down.

CHAPTER THIRTY-ONE

Ernie Smith. Remember him? The newt finder.

Unlike most of the protestors, Ernie had no particular attachment to Ravenwood. He was only here because his bedroom overlooked the village main street, and the sound of the gathering protestors cycling past his window had woken him. Never one to be left out, he had followed, and now here he was.

On a branch, in a tree, above the tree house.

He had sung, he had chanted, he had waved signs, but now he was bored. Too much talking, too many grown-ups, too much sitting still when what he really wanted (Raffy could have told you this) was to play football.

So Ernie wriggled. Something dug into his back. He wriggled again and rolled his head, glancing up . . .

Just as the nuthatch hopped out of its hollow.

For a few seconds, Ernie gazed at it. Not being a bird-loving sort of boy, he had paid as little attention to nuthatches in his nine years as he had to newts, but now that he saw one up close he knew he would never forget it. It was so funny, with its blue-grey wings folded like a fancy coat over its plump buff breast! So *cool*, with that black stripe right across its face, over its eyes like a bandit's mask!

Why had no one ever told him that birds were cool?

After a while, though, he grew bored again. Looking at a nuthatch might have been enough for most people, but not for Ernie Smith. Ernie wanted more. Specifically, Ernie wanted to see where the nuthatch lived, in the little hollow a few metres above his head.

And so Ernie got up and stood on tiptoe
and Ernie slipped
Ernie screamed
and Ernie fell.

The tree house broke his fall, as did the platform, and the branches beneath. He was lucky to fall partly on the mattress, hastily vacated by the grown-up protestors. But for almost a minute after he fell, he lost consciousness. And when he came round, he could not move his arm.

All the oxygen was sucked out of the fight. One by one, the appalled grown-ups got to their feet to offer help. Martha, who had run out of the house when she heard Ernie scream, called his mother. Nick drove him back to the village. The others followed, a little shame-faced. The children of Ashby-under-Raven stayed in Yggdrasil a little longer, waiting while Leo conversed with Alex and Jack by the raven gate. Some of them still hoped, when he left his brothers to return to Yggdrasil, that all was not yet lost. But before he even spoke, one look at his ashen face told them it was over.

Leo did not look at the children as they left, but stood facing away from them over the meadow, still shaking with the knowledge that a child was badly hurt, and that like the fire it had happened on his watch.

*

From the woods, Noa heard the cheer go up for Leo. She hoped this meant that they had won, but she did not return to Yggdrasil. This was not her victory.

The sheer loneliness of it brought a lump to her throat. To stop herself crying, she picked up the stick Raffy had left on the pontoon, just over a week ago on the morning Bea had left, and jabbed it into the pond, right to the bottom, so that mud swirled. It made her feel strangely better. She jabbed again. And froze.

There was something in the water.

The next jab was more of a gentle poke, cautious, in case she was wrong. She leaned forward, still unsure ...

She leaned further.

CRACK!

A sound like a gunshot ripped through the woods as the old pontoon finally gave way. Noa cried out as she fell, but no one heard her. Then the cold dark water closed over her head.

CHAPTER THIRTY-TWO

In the kitchen, Leo wept in Martha's arms.

'I'm sorry,' he said, as she held him close. 'I'm so sorry. I so nearly told my brothers I wouldn't sell, but Ernie...'

'I know,' said Martha.

'He could have broken his neck.'

'But he didn't.' She took his face in her hands. 'It will be all right,' she said.

'How?' asked Leo. 'You know what Ernie's fall means, don't you? If Alex and Ingrid had any doubts about Bea going to live with them before, they won't now. They already thought the fire was my fault, and now this!'

'But it's *not* your fault,' said Martha. 'It's not, Leo.

They want you to think you're irresponsible because it suits them. You're a good man, Leo, and your niece and my son are a credit to you. I understand, my love, why you agreed to sell Ravenwood. I understand we can't afford to maintain it without Alex's help, but don't let them make you believe you've done anything wrong, because you haven't.'

Leo shuddered and wrapped his arms around her. For a few seconds, they stood without talking.

'We'll make it all right, won't we? Wherever we live next, we'll make it work.'

'Of course we will,' said Martha bravely. 'We'll get a mortgage, and we'll buy somewhere, and Bea will come for holidays and Raffy will be fine and it will all work out.'

Leo held her a little longer, trying to convince himself that she was right. Then, with a groan, he let her go.

'Oh, but Martha,' he said. '*Ygg* . . .'

Bea and Raffy had waited until everyone else had climbed down from Yggdrasil, then pulled up the ladder and begun to climb. Now they sat on branches high above the tree house while Grandma watched with interest from Martha's favourite bench, Ant and Jack conversed by the raven gate, Colin the tree man napped in his van and Alex shouted at his daughter.

What do you think you are going to achieve can't you see what you're doing to your mother this is ridiculous Bea will you answer me look I have loved this tree too but what's done is done and at the end of the day it is just a tree . . .

'Just ignore him,' Bea said to Raffy. 'I am. Listen to him! *What you're doing to your mother* – Mum was completely up for protesting. I had no idea she could be so cool.'

Don't say I didn't warn you Bea I am going to get a ladder and carry you down myself . . .

Raffy, unsure how he felt about Ingrid being cool, peered down at the ground.

'He's going to the barn with Jack.'

Bea leaned back against the trunk and closed her eyes.

'Let him,' she said. 'There's no ladder at Ravenwood long enough to reach us here.'

Raffy grunted and wriggled into a more

comfortable position, catlike on his belly along a branch, laying his cheek on the cool bark.

'Do you think Noa's all right?' he asked. 'Where did she go?'

'I don't know if she's all right. She went to the woods to hide, I think, because she's convinced everything is her fault. We'll have to be very nice to her, when all of this is over. I don't think it's enough to just tell her we forgive her, we have to show her we really love her. But for now, let's just stay here as long as we can.'

'How long will that be?'

'Until we get too hungry, I suppose.'

And so, probably for the last time, they sat quietly in the old ash tree. Through Yggdrasil's strong, elegant branches, the sky was a bright, serene blue but a gentle breeze wafted through its long-fingered leaves.

They both knew that if they could only stay like this forever, they would be forever happy. It was a perfect summer day.

But all too soon, there was the sound of voices below, followed by clanging and thumping as a ladder was let out then propped against Ygg's trunk, then Alex again.

I'm coming up this is your final warning Beatrice will you answer me!

They ignored him as long as they could, but as his voice grew nearer it became harder and harder to pretend he wasn't there.

But then . . .

'Darling, please! Oh, Alex, be careful!'

Bea and Raffy both looked down.

Alex was gripping the ladder very hard with both hands. He looked up and Bea saw that he was sweating, and very red in the face. At the foot of the tree, Ingrid was following his progress with her hands over her face, peeping through her fingers.

'Is he scared of heights?' Raffy curled his lip. 'I thought he was always playing in Ygg when he was our age. That's what Leo says.'

Bea rolled her eyes. 'Maybe that's what happens when you get old.'

She really, *really* didn't want to feel sorry for her father.

Alex whimpered as he took another step. Ingrid cried out.

'Bea, darling, do something! He's going to fall.'

Bea sighed.

'You said to ignore them,' said Raffy, desperate for a bit more time.

'I know,' said Bea. 'But the stupid idiot might actually hurt himself.'

It really was over.

Raffy first, then Bea, climbed back down to the tree house. There, as slowly as possible, they gathered everything into the pulley basket – the plates and mugs Martha had given them, their duvets from last night, the bucket. When everything was packed, they lowered the basket then threw down the rope pulley.

Before leaving, Raffy went over to the window, finished only four days ago by him and Noa and Nick. Beneath him spread the meadow, the hillside, the woods. The valley. The sea.

Their whole world.

'What would they think, the people who planted Ygg?' he asked.

'They'd be baffled,' said Bea. 'Also, furious.'

'*I'm* baffled and furious.'

'Yeah. Me too.'

One last pat of the excellent tree house. One last stroke of the branches which held it, one last glance at the soon to be homeless nuthatch. One last pressing of cheeks to the old gnarled bark. One last hug of the trunk when they reached the ground where they gathered up their belongings. Then, hand in hand and with tears rolling down their cheeks, ignoring Alex and Ingrid and without a backward glance, they walked towards the house where Leo and Martha were waiting for them.

Behind them, the whine of a chainsaw started up.

Raffy stopped.

'Don't turn round,' said Bea. 'Don't you dare look.'

'I can't help it,' said Raffy. 'I have to. Bea, he's walking up to Ygg now. He's about to . . .'

'STOP!'

'Noa?' Bea spun round. Raffy too. Yes, there was Noa – running across the meadow towards Yggdrasil from the woods, dripping wet and streaked with mud. They watched in amazement as she stumbled up to the old ash and threw herself at Colin's feet.

'What the . . .?' Colin stepped back and turned off the chainsaw, as one by one Martha and Leo, Bea and Raffy began to run towards them.

At the foot of Yggdrasil, Noa, panting, almost crying, reached into her pocket.

'I was at the pond. I found something!'

'Oh my God!' Bea began to laugh hysterically. 'Oh my God, please tell me you found a newt! A Protected Newt Which Means They Can't Build!'

Raffy gave her an injured look.

'There *is* no newt,' he said. 'If there was, I would have found it.'

'It's not a newt,' said Noa.

And she opened her hand.

CHAPTER THIRTY-THREE

They were all there now, at the foot of Yggdrasil. Bea, Raffy, Martha, Leo. Colin, Ant, Alex, Ingrid. Noa. Grandma. Jack.

All there, and staring at the heavy rectangular object in Noa's palm.

'I don't understand,' said Ingrid.

'It's my lighter,' said Jack, with a frown. 'I lost it a few days ago. Where on Earth did you find it?'

'In the pond,' said Noa.

'In the *pond*?'

Martha had picked up one of the duvets Bea and Raffy had sent down from the tree house. She draped it around Noa's shoulders now, asking, 'What were you doing at the pond?'

Noa squirmed. 'I didn't want to stay at the protest,' she muttered. 'I didn't think it was right, because of the fire, because I thought it was all my fault...'

'Oh, Noa,' said Leo.

'... but now I know it wasn't, because of the lighter.'

With a great effort, Noa raised her chin to look directly at Jack.

'Well, don't ask *me* what she means!' he said, as everyone turned towards him. 'I have no idea what she's talking about, or how my lighter ended up in the pond. Thank you for finding it, Noa. I wish you hadn't risked drowning, but I'm grateful to have it back.'

He reached out for the lighter.

Noa stepped away.

'Oh, for heaven's sake, child!' snapped Grandma. 'All this drama's not good for an old woman. Just spit out what's on your mind.'

Noa opened her mouth, then closed it again. She had been so sure when she found the lighter, but what if she was wrong?

'Just say it straight,' advised Martha.

Noa took a shaky breath and tried to reason with herself. If she was wrong, things wouldn't get much worse for her. They might all think she was a bit desperate, but then she *felt* desperate. And Jack might hate her, but she didn't really care about that.

And if she was right . . .

If she was right, she would be able to sleep again.

She raised her chin. Where to begin?

'I was doing this drawing . . .'

'Oh, what *is* this!' cried Jack. 'What is she talking about, a drawing?'

Noa faltered.

'Go on,' said Martha, with a frown to silence Jack.

Noa started again.

'I was doing this drawing, and Jack was smoking, and he used a match . . . and it just . . . I mean, it made me realise . . . I mean, it's just that Jack always uses his lighter. He said so, on our first night. But then after the fire he started using matches . . . because his lighter was in the pond . . .' She tailed off, mumbling. Everyone was staring at her, all looking different variations of puzzled.

'I'm not sure I understand,' said Leo.

'After the fire, he started using matches . . .' Raffy repeated. *After the fire he started using matches . . .*

Bea gasped. 'He used the lighter to start the fire!' she cried. 'Then threw it away to hide the evidence!'

Ingrid clapped her hand over her mouth.

Jack narrowed his eyes.

'Really, Bea!' said Alex. 'Must you be so dramatic?'

Bea glared at him. 'Yes,' she said. 'I must.'

'The lighter likely just fell out of his pocket.' Ant frowned, like he was trying to be understanding but also struggling to be patient. 'It's not evidence of anything. Now if everyone could step back again, Colin has a job to . . .'

'It can't have,' Raffy interrupted.

'What can't have what?' sighed Ant.

'The lighter can't have just fallen out of Jack's pocket.' Raffy held out his hand to Noa. After a short hesitation, she gave it to him and he shoved it in his pocket. Then, to everyone's astonishment, he did a forward roll. When he was upright again, he pulled the lighter triumphantly out of his pocket.

Bea gave a second gasp.

'And your point is?' asked Jack.

'Things *don't* just fall out of pockets,' Raffy explained. 'Especially into ponds. Jack would have had to be standing on his head right on the edge of the pontoon or something, for that to happen.'

Leo frowned and patted his own pockets, like he was trying to work out how easily things would fall out of them.

'Oh, this is absurd!' cried Alex. 'Noa, I get how hard the fire hit you and I can understand you wanting to shift the blame . . .'

'Alex,' said Ingrid.

'What? I'm not saying the fire was the kid's *fault* . . .'

'Just stop.'

'It's not true, Jack, is it?' asked Leo.

As Jack turned towards Leo, his gaze swept over the children. Bea shivered. She had never seen anyone look so . . . what was it?

Sad. Yes, sad. But how did that fit with what Noa was saying?

'I can't actually believe you're asking me that,' Jack said. 'Yes, I want to sell Ravenwood. But set fire to it? Ravenwood was my *home*, Leo. I may not love it like you do, but *burn it*? The place I grew up, where *we* grew up, together?'

The brothers looked at each other, and as they did Bea saw them differently. Not as grown men who gave orders and made stupid decisions but as children, playing in and around Ravenwood just like Raffy and Noa and her.

'He didn't do it,' she whispered to the others.

Disappointed, all three of them hung their heads.

'But the *lighter*,' whispered Raffy. '*Someone* must have thrown it.'

Understanding hit Noa like a blow to the chest.

'Ant,' she said, and her voice was so strong it seemed to ring in her ears. 'Ant did it. He's the one who started the fire.'

CHAPTER THIRTY-FOUR

Ant's laughter had a hard edge that wasn't funny. 'Why would *I* start a fire?'

'For everything that happened afterwards.' Noa, reeling from shock, dug her heels into the ground to steady herself. 'To make Leo agree to sell.'

'That's insane.'

'Is it?' Leo said slowly.

'Leo!' said Alex. 'You're surely not going along with this? Noa, be very careful. You can't just go around accusing . . .'

'Alex,' said Ingrid again.

Noa looked at her gratefully and pressed on.

'Everything started to change after Ant got here. First, Bea went away . . .'

'Bea went away before Ant got here,' said Jack.

'But *after* Ant said he was interested in buying Ravenwood,' Raffy breathed. 'That's why Bea's parents invited her. Leo told Mum. They wanted to make sure they liked her before selling Ravenwood and asking her to live with them.'

Ingrid winced.

'That's not *exactly* how it happened,' muttered Alex.

'Isn't it?' demanded Bea.

'And then Raffy went to London . . .' said Noa.

'This is ridiculous,' said Ant. 'I'm not going to stand by while a twelve-year-old . . .'

'Eleven,' said Bea coldly.

'What?'

'She's eleven.'

'Whatever. While a little kid spouts nonsense. What the hell did I have to do with anyone going to London?'

But Raffy was on a roll now. 'You knew about Grandma, didn't you?' he said. 'At dinner, that time, when you asked all those questions about Mum's family. Didn't you? But how?'

Jack scratched the ground with his foot.

'Jack!' said Leo.

'Leo!' said Martha.

'I told him ages ago, in confidence.' Leo gave his brother a reproachful stare. 'Before he turned into a snake.'

'Did *everyone* know about Grandma except me?' asked Raffy.

'Only the grown-ups,' growled Bea.

'Right.' Ant crossed his arms. 'So I asked Martha about her family. How was I to know they'd hare off to London?'

'You weren't,' Noa admitted. Her mind was racing. It was all falling into place, but she had to get this right, or Ant would slip away. 'But you're clever, you knew you were upsetting them. That's what you do. You *destabilise*. You make people question themselves, so they don't focus on what's right in front of them. That's how you win. Leo begged Martha not to go away while you were here. I heard him. I didn't understand then but I do now. He needed Martha because she makes him strong.'

Leo reached for Martha's hand. 'That's true enough.'

'But after you asked Martha about her family, Raffy had questions.' Words were tumbling out of Noa now, so fast she could barely keep up with them. 'And rather than stay she put him first, because that is what *good* parents do. And it all worked out perfectly for you, didn't it? With Martha gone, Leo was much more likely to give in. All you needed was to give a final push, which was the fire, which then ...' Noa was pressing her heels so hard her knees were beginning to hurt. 'Which then, you made me think was my fault.'

'I did not!' A vein was throbbing dangerously at Ant's temple. 'What I *said* was, accidents happen and ...'

'And I fell for it.' Ingrid had gone very pale. 'I wasn't sure about Bea coming to live with us, but when I thought it wasn't safe here any more that made up my mind. That's when Alex decided to sell ...'

'... and I agreed as well.' Leo looked at Ant with dislike.

Ant's suntan had gone from orange to a rather ugly shade of purple.

'For God's sake,' he protested. 'I was the first to try to put out the fire!'

'Because you were first on the scene,' said Noa. 'And that's something else that doesn't make sense. Why *were* you there?'

'I wanted to stretch my legs!' Ant was sounding more and more defensive. 'We'd had a long drive, we'd been out to visit a hotel on the other side of York.'

'Oh, *really*!' Noa shook with rage now, as the events of the night began to flood back. All this time, thinking she was the culprit! All the nightmares, and the feeling she didn't belong, worrying that people could have *died* because of her! 'Well, I remember exactly what happened. I was in Skidbládnir. I was playing with the lantern, I do admit that. I was throwing shadows across the grass. That's when I heard your car come back, but then there was the owl . . .'

'Dear me,' said Grandma. 'Now there's an owl.'

'I saw the owl and it was amazing, but then *I put the lantern away*. I know I did. After the fire I was confused and I thought maybe I didn't, but I

323

remember now, because the latch on the locker was stiff. And *you* . . . you must have seen me from the car. You waited till I was gone, and you thought . . .' She turned to Jack. 'When did you notice your lighter was missing?'

'That evening,' Jack admitted. 'I had a smoke in the car coming home from York. I used the lighter then, and I put it in the tray by the gear stick because it was too tight putting it back in my jeans pocket. And I haven't seen it since.'

'Doesn't make me an arsonist,' snarled Ant.

'You probably didn't mean for the fire to get so big,' said Noa fairly. 'But everything was so dry after the drought it got out of control. Not that I suppose you mind that much. You don't care about the cost of things, you're the sort of person who always wants their own way.'

Ant laughed. 'Isn't everyone?'

Nobody laughed with him.

'Oh for God's sake, you don't believe this kid, do you?'

Alex said, 'I think you'd better leave.'

CHAPTER THIRTY-FIVE

So the deal with Ant was off and Yggdrasil was saved.

Ant and Colin departed, without goodbyes. Martha ushered everyone else towards the house. As they walked across the meadow, Bea threw her arms around Noa and told her she had been amazing.

'The way you stood up to him! The way you didn't let him bully you! The way you worked it all out! I *knew* that story with the lantern didn't make sense! Didn't I always say?'

Noa wriggled away, trying to pretend she wasn't delighted with herself.

'I owe you an apology, Noa,' said Leo. 'I let you believe you started the fire, and it was deeply unfair.

You must regret ever coming to Ravenwood.'

'Regret coming to Ravenwood!' cried Bea. 'Noa *adores* Ravenwood, don't you, Noa? She's one of us now.'

Noa stopped trying to pretend and beamed. Leo grinned.

'Well, whatever you think of Ravenwood, Noa, you were splendid back there, absolutely splendid.'

'You were *all* splendid,' said Ingrid, though it was clear by the way she looked at Bea who she considered the most splendid of all.

'Apart from the small matter of running away from Venice,' said Alex.

'And from Kings Cross,' said Martha, with feeling.

'And from Kings Cross,' Alex agreed. 'Do I need to ask how you actually managed it?'

'I think probably not,' said Bea. 'Though we do owe Noa's sister for the Eurostar ticket.'

'Of course we do,' said Alex, rolling his eyes but smiling.

They arrived at the terrace. The grown-ups settled on the broken chairs, with Grandma on the bench and Noa between Bea and Raffy on the steps. When

Leo and Martha had brought out tea, Alex cleared his throat to speak.

'We ought really to talk about what happens next.'

They all turned to stare at him.

'Well, it's not *over*,' he said. 'None of the issues which have brought us here have actually been resolved. All that's happened is that we've lost a buyer. I'm glad, because I don't want to sell Ravenwood to a man like that. But the fact remains that Jack still wants to sell his share.' Alex faltered, casting a sideways glance at Bea. 'And so, maybe, do we.'

'I don't *want* to sell Ravenwood,' said Jack, who until now had been very quiet. 'If I could afford to, I'd keep it. And Noa, I'm sorry. It's me who owes you the biggest apology, not Leo. I wanted the deal with Ant to work so badly I was blinded. I mean, even when he said he wanted to cut down Ygg ... I can't believe I was prepared to go through with it. If I could, I'd just sell my third of Ravenwood, but who wants to buy a third of a house?'

'I would,' said Martha.

Jack brightened. 'Really?'

'But I can't afford to.'

'So that's that, then,' said Leo. 'We look for another buyer.'

Bea's parents, her uncles and Martha drank their tea, looking defeated. Grandma, alone on her bench, gazed thoughtfully at the slug trails on a clump of lupins in the flower bed beside her.

'I wonder,' she said, 'if you have a hedgehog.'

Martha rubbed her face wearily. 'What?'

'A hedgehog would eat the snails.'

'Mum, I'm not sure this is the time . . .'

'Of course,' said Grandma, and the grown-ups once again were quiet.

'What, so it's all been for nothing?' Raffy was beginning to feel a new urge to kick something. 'Bea running away from Italy and us running away from London and Noa almost drowning and Ernie nearly breaking his neck . . .'

'It's not for nothing,' insisted Martha. 'You saved Yggdrasil! You were amazing!'

'But I won't be able to *see* Ygg if we move!' Raffy, for want of anything to kick, stamped his foot. 'You don't understand! None of you understand! You just take everything away, like it's nothing! All your

328

talk about bats and meadows and butterflies and birds. It's not fair to make us love them and believe they're the most important thing in the world if you're just prepared to sell them to someone who doesn't care about them. It wasn't just Jack who was ready to sell, it was *all* of you. Leo agreed, and Alex agreed, and *you* didn't really try to stop them, Mum, you just said there was nothing you could do. You say we'll find somewhere else to live and everything will be all right, but you don't understand what you're taking from us.'

Martha opened her mouth to protest. Then, thinking better of it, closed it again.

'Of course it *will* be all right, in a way.' Noa went a very dark red, as everyone turned towards her (except Grandma, now sharing crumbs of digestive biscuits with a robin). 'Things are, usually. I mean, you get used to them, even if with all your might you wish they hadn't changed. It doesn't mean things don't hurt.'

She reached for Raffy and Bea's hands. They shuffled closer to each other on the step and glowered at the adults.

'What you have to understand,' said Bea, 'is that Ravenwood isn't just a place, it's *us*. It's like …' She paused as a gust of wind blew a lock of hair across her face. 'Me and Raffy, we've been here since we were babies. It's like we're *made* of Ravenwood. Maybe it was the same for Leo and Jack and Dad when you were our age, I don't know. I guess things change when you're old, like Dad getting vertigo climbing Ygg, because if you felt like we do you *couldn't* sell Ravenwood. It would be like trying to … like trying to sell your own blood! What none of you seem to understand is that places matter. Where we *come* from matters. It's no good pretending they don't.'

In the short silence that followed, Grandma cleared her throat.

'I wonder,' she said, 'if I can help.'

CHAPTER THIRTY-SIX

'I don't know what Bea's parents will decide to do,' said Grandma. 'But I will buy Jack's share of Ravenwood.'

'You?' cried Jack.

'Yes, me.' Grandma fixed him with a withering stare. 'Do you think I can't afford it? I can, you know. Or at least I will be able to when I've sold some of Joe's paintings.'

Martha's mouth dropped open.

'Oh, don't look at me like that, child,' grumbled Grandma.

'But you love those paintings!'

'No, I don't, I loved your father. I can still love him without those great big canvases depressing me every time I look at them. Do you know what he would have done today, Martha, if he had been here? He would have been up in that tree, chanting louder than any of the others. He was passionate about forests, he hated to see what is happening to them all over the world. The Amazon, the Congo, our own woodlands. Why do you think he painted them broken? And what sense is there in keeping his work in a poky flat, if it can be of use? When I could be using the money from selling it to save a real woodland?'

Raffy began to smile as she glared round at the assembled company. He rather loved his peculiar grandmother.

'I have conditions, though.'

Grandma settled back on the bench and began to count on her fingers, clearly enjoying herself.

'One. I had a good poke around the house when Martha showed me to the bathroom. It's a good house, but it must be repaired. There's a hole in the ceiling of one of the bedrooms.'

'It's on my list,' said Leo, somewhat defensively.

Grandma frowned at him. 'Lists aren't good

enough. There should not be holes in ceilings. Two . . .' She waved towards the meadow. 'All of this is a waste of space.'

Leo spluttered.

'Oh, I know what you are going to say! Nature, birds, butterflies – I don't mean *that*. I do *know* about biodiversity.'

Bea and Raffy grinned at each other.

'The waste of space I refer to are those barns. Three of them, empty!'

'One of them is my studio!' Leo objected.

'Two empty barns, then. And my second condition is this. That those barns be converted into studios for local artists. We will charge them rent, of course, but not much – enough to cover bills and maintenance and so forth. We will call the barn complex the Joe Drori Art Centre. There will be a small exhibition space, and also workshops for children. It will be a way of supporting and encouraging new artists, and it will be my husband's legacy.' Another glare. 'I will pay for the conversion. Leo will manage the artists. For this he will be paid, though not much.'

Leo gave a rueful smile. 'Fair.'

'Three. I will not buy this share of Ravenwood for myself but for my daughter, Martha Drori, and for my grandson, Rafael Joseph Drori. This is their home. I won't have anyone selling it without their consent.'

Martha's eyes had gone very shiny. 'Mum, you really don't have to . . .'

'Oh, hush, child! The paintings will go to you anyway when I die. Let's make use of them while I'm alive! Four, I want my own bedroom. I shan't live here, but I want to come and go as I please. Families . . .' Here Grandma took a breath to steady her voice. 'Families shouldn't be apart, not when they miss each other as I have missed mine.'

'Oh, Mum . . .'

She darted away from Leo to kiss her mother. Grandma blinked and patted her hand, before turning to Raffy. 'Come along, Rafael, and show me these woods and cliffs of yours, while we let these people discuss my offer. Noa, come with us. Beatrice, I believe you need to talk to your parents. Even if Jack does sell to me, there is still the question of your father's share.'

Grandma, Raffy and Noa left, leaving behind a stunned silence.

'Well!' said Martha at last. 'I was not expecting that!'

Jack, looking dazed, said, 'Do you think she means it?'

'My mother rarely says anything she doesn't mean,' said Martha.

'And are you happy for us to accept?' asked Leo hopefully. 'We won't do it if you're not.'

'I will!' said Jack.

Martha laughed. 'Do you know, I *am* happy. I am very happy indeed.'

'Which just leaves Alex.' Leo turned to his older brother. 'What are you going to do?'

'That,' said Alex, 'rather depends on Bea.'

Bea and her parents walked to the edge of the cliff and sat on the ground by the sad remains of Skidbládnir to talk.

They started at the beginning, eleven years ago, on the morning after the storm, when Alex first brought Bea to Ravenwood, because the childminder was sick and Ingrid was having one of her bad days.

'I was so ill after you were born,' Ingrid whispered. 'Physically at first, but afterwards, in my head. I couldn't stop crying. I thought I could never be a good mother to you, the mother you deserved. And Dad and I were both so tired. It was only meant to be for a few days. I thought, just a little rest and I would be better but oh, darling, the world just felt so *dark* …'

The goldfinches flitted in the meadow behind them, the skylarks sang, the swallows and house martins wheeled. Ingrid talked on and on – about dark days when she couldn't get out of bed, and better days when she hoped she could become the mother she wanted to be. About how Alex had tried to tell her nobody knew how to be a parent, that probably they had to learn as they went along. About how she wanted to believe him. Alex blew his nose rather loudly at that point, and Ingrid started to cry.

'I'm sorry, I'm sorry, I'm sorry,' she wept. 'I wanted so much … Bea, there's not a day went by when I didn't love you and want you with me. But you were so happy at Ravenwood … That's why we didn't want to sell it, you know that? It's why we needed to be absolutely sure ... But do you think now, darling – now that we've spent time together, now that you know, now that I *am* better – I can feel it, now that I am stronger – do you think you *could* live with us?'

Ingrid reached for Alex's hand and clung to it, while Bea hugged her knees to her chest and thought.

She thought of Venice, of that happy week on the *Carolina*, and how she had always longed for her parents' love and approval. She thought of poor Ingrid and her darkness. She didn't understand exactly what it was, this illness of her mother's, but she understood that she *had* been ill, and that she was brave. She thought about the word *home* and what that meant.

Which would it be – Ravenwood, or London?

The raven, with a loud caw, took wing and soared out above the cove. Bea watched it go. How nice to be a bird, she thought, and to not have to make such choices ...

Bea began to smile. Life was full of choices. Hadn't she said as much to Leo, last night? And hadn't Raffy's grandmother just proved it?

'What are you thinking, Bea?' asked Alex. 'I don't want to rush you, but it *would* be nice to know.'

Bea turned to her parents and beamed.

'I have a different plan,' she said.

And so it was settled. Bea refused to choose Ravenwood *or* London, but decided that instead she wanted both. She would make Ravenwood her main home, and go to school at Meadowbanks in the autumn as planned. But Ingrid and Alex would visit more often and for longer, and there would be more trips to London to see them, and whenever Alex could he would work from Ravenwood, so that visits weren't just in the holidays but took place all year round. It was a compromise, but one which made everyone happy, and the grown-ups decided there should be a picnic at the cove to celebrate.

In the flurry of activity to prepare for it, unlikely partnerships were born. Alex and Martha drove to the shop. Ingrid and Grandma baked. Jack and Leo roamed about gathering parasols and blankets and all the other things necessary for a special occasion.

The three children, apparently in the way, retreated to Yggdrasil and sat on the old platform with their legs dangling over the edge to talk.

'Did Ingrid cry too?' Raffy had sobbed with relief when Bea told him about her plan

'Of course,' said Bea. 'But then she was pleased, especially when I told her I don't care if she cries. I explained I'd rather have a crying mum than none at all – that really set her off, and Dad. Honestly, the pair of them! Anyway, they've cancelled the Italian villa and they're going to spend the rest of the holiday here. Dad's going to buy a boat.'

'A *yacht*?'

'Well, no. An inflatable canoe. But it's a start! Raffy, what about your grandmother? How is it going to be with her here? Because even I think she's a bit scary.'

'She isn't really,' said Raffy. 'I actually like her. Mainly, I think she's lonely.'

'Not any more, though.'

Raffy grunted. 'It's nice to have more family. And Mum's pleased too, because you know secretly I think she's quite a London person. I mean, she was mega stressed the whole time we were there, but you could tell she liked it. So maybe we'll go to London more too.'

'So everything changes but everything stays the same,' said Bea happily. 'And we can go back to having the best summer ever. The best summer ever, and then ... school. It'll be your turn to show us round then, Noa, when we go to town every day. Noa! Stop looking at your phone!'

Noa smiled. It *would* be nice to start school with friends.

'The best summer ever sounds good,' she said. 'But first I need to send a message. Your grandmother was right, Raffy. Families shouldn't be apart, not when they miss each other.'

EPILOGUE

I t was the sort of picnic you read about in books.

There was a chair and a parasol for Grandma on the sand, there were bright rugs laid out beside her, proper china and a cool box for drinks in the shade. They didn't dare light a fire for a barbecue, but there were chicken drumsticks roasted in a sticky sauce, there were sausages and salads and strawberries, Grandma's meringues like puffy sweet clouds and a pineapple upside-down cake made by Ingrid. The tide was too low for cliff-jumping, but there were swimming races, and competitions to see who could dive the deepest, and when the beach was at its widest there were ball games on the sand.

There was Ingrid and Bea walking on the sand,

there was Martha sitting with Grandma. There were three brothers swimming together to the mouth of the cove as they used to when they were boys, and there was Raffy with a snorkel and mask unearthed from the barn, hoping to find a rare fish.

There was Noa, watching the path, and there was the moment when her heart stopped because there at the top of the cliff where Skidbládnir used to sit was the familiar silhouette of her father, and behind him the figures of a woman and two little girls . . .

There was Noa running into the water with her father, not stopping to check for the cold, and there was Bea and Raffy going in after them, each holding a squealing, happy twin.

Later, when Noa's father, Tamsin and the twins had left, when Martha had taken Grandma upstairs to the bedroom Jack had vacated for her and the three brothers had driven to the village to fetch fish and chips, the three children went back to Yggdrasil.

In due course, the summer of Ravenwood's rescue would pass into family legend, right up there with the wars and the fires which had destroyed it in the past. But for now, there was no need to talk about any of that. Noa lay on her front on the platform watching her dad's car bounce down the lane, and thought about the private conversation she had had with him in the woods, and how good it had felt to tell him the truth about how angry she had been with him for leaving, and how lonely she had been since he left. But maybe, she had said, when the new term starts, she could come and stay one weekend. Dad had hugged her very close when she said that. Then, when Noa had felt in her pocket and pulled out a dried-out ash key which she pressed into his hand, he had laughed.

'What's this, then?' he had asked, and Noa had replied, 'A promise.'

Above Noa, perched on the tree-house roof, Raffy was deeply at peace. How afraid he had been, a few days ago, to ask Martha why he had come to Ravenwood! Well, he *had* asked, and look what had happened as a result! Ravenwood saved, everyone happy! As he gazed up into the green long-fingered branches, Raffy thought – no, he was sure – that he felt the spirit of the ancient ash thanking him.

Bea, lying on her bunk inside the treehouse, was thinking many things. She thought a bit about Venice and a bit about London, a bit about Alex and a lot about Ingrid. She thought about Josh and how to get a message to him that Ravenwood was saved, she cursed the woman who had stolen the piece of paper with the major's phone number, she wondered if she could track him down online to thank him. She thought about the mountains of Switzerland she would one day go and see in daylight, and about the two girls living under a staircase in Paris, hoping they were safe and would soon find a proper home. And then her mind let go of all these things, and focused on more immediate things.

'I wonder,' she called through the open door.

'What?' Raffy's head appeared upside down from the roof.

'Do you think we could sleep up here every night until the end of the holidays?' asked Bea.

'We'd need better lighting,' said Noa. '*Not* fire-based.'

'And we should put up a curtain around the wee bucket,' said Raffy.

'And make a locker for snacks that animals can't get into ...' said Bea.

On and on they talked, making plans for their perfect Ravenwood summer. Above them, oblivious to the danger which had so nearly befallen it, the nuthatch bashed an acorn on a branch, while in the cove, with no one watching, a solitary seal swam beneath the calling ravens.

More Natasha Farrant
adventures are waiting . . .

24-03-23

PILLGWENLLY

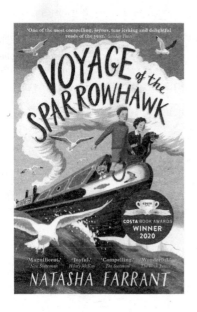

**WINNER – COSTA
BOOK AWARD**

Join Lotti, Ben, Clara and a
growing number of dogs on
a daring journey in search of
lost loved ones and a place
to call home . . .

Join Alice on a epic quest
across wild Scottish
highlands and islands,
where friendships will
be made and broken, lies
will be untangled and the
children will face danger and
excitement at every turn . . .

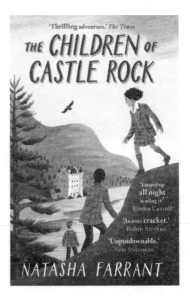